Speaking with The
Almighty
The messages of the
Book of Deuteronomy
(Speaking with The
Celestial Guide)

DEDICATION

This book is dedicated to my loving family and friends.

The messages contained within this book are based on reading the Book of Deuteronomy through a magnifying glass.

The book is called "Deuteronomy" because according to scholars, there were two laws given in the wilderness: God's Law ("decree") and Moses' Law; hence the Koine Greek name from the Septeguinst ("Seventy") translation of the book which entered the Vulgata, The Latin Translation of the Bible (still in use in the Roman Catholic Church) from Deuteronomion, literally "second law," from deuteros "second" (see deutero-) + nomos "law" (from PIE root *nem- "assign, allot; take").

The original Jewish name for the book is "Dvarim", which means "Words" and has a second name among religious scholars – "Torat Moshe" or "Moses' Law".

The critique (if any) presented here is mine and mine only, and there is no added text from any kind of modern or ancient source which may critique parts of the bible based on different ecclesiastical views.

The passages quoted within this text are taken from the King James Version of the Bible, chosen for being the closest text resembling the original Hebrew version of the Old Testament.

No alterations exist within the ancient text presented here.

ACKNOWLEDGMENTS

ACKNOWLEDGMENTS

I would like to thank my wife for her undying support of me in my hardships, even before reading this book and to thank my dear son for helping me with the creation of this book and its translation into different languages.

The First Message – Prelude

Enoch: Thank you for getting back to me.

The Celestial Guide: The messages I am about to give you are as valid today as they were millennia ago.

Enoch: Is Deuteronomy the continuance of the Book of Numbers?

TCG: One could say that, yes. But it is a lot more than just a continuance; it is an assortment of laws and teachings which overshadow what was written in Numbers.

Enoch: What do you mean by that?

TCG: It gives more of a background of what was written in the earlier books as well a more in-depth interpretation of the teachings given there.

Enoch: I don't I follow.

TCG: What happened first, the chicken or the egg? Is it possible that despite covering everything which was written in the previous books, Deuteronomy precedes them...?

Enoch: That's impossible, at least chronologically speaking.

TCG: Maybe, but there may have been a literary manipulation to make it seem so. Let's move on and delve into that later.

Enoch: I am ready.

TCG: *"These be the words which Moses spake unto all Israel on this side Jordan in the wilderness, in the plain over against the Red sea, between Paran, and Tophel, and Laban, and Hazeroth, and Dizahab."* (Deuteronomy 1, 1)

This is why the name of the book in Hebrew is "Words", these are not God's words but Moses', with God not intervening in Moses' decisions. There was an ecclesiastical author who wrote everything that Moses had said as truth. Moses is the hero here.

Enoch: Interesting, so this is like Kurosawa's Rashomon? There's a hero with some interpretation of what happened and other heroes are saying what they think happened in turn.

TCG: Pretty much, yes.

Enoch: How so? Is this like a summary of what he had done for the Israelites before he died?

TCG: Maybe, but he wasn't departing just yet.

Enoch: And what do you surmise of this?

TCG: God had already told Moses he was about to die, so Moses decided to speak of the Leadership of the Israelites in the future. God had kept Moses alive while anointing Joshua under him, as God had so decreed.

There were skirmishes and wars in the meantime, while the Israelites were hindered in the Transjordan. It may have been Moses' wish or "hope" if you will, that God was still in need of him...?

Joshua kept silent at that stage, and God was not speaking to him yet.

To be honest, God had never spoken to Joshua before.

Enoch: So what's going on here?

TCG: Moses told the Israelites everything they have endured in their lives; most of them were the people of the desert – their parents already died in the wilderness: *"And it came to pass in the fortieth year, in the eleventh month, on the first day of the month, that Moses spake unto the children of Israel, according unto all that the LORD had given him in commandment unto them."* (Deuteronomy 1, 3) The author cannot contain himself and writes it as if these <u>were God's words</u> unto the Israelites. But the Israelites had felt that Moses was their undisputed champion. But, as we remember Moses, he cannot save the tirade from the people of what <u>he endured</u> because of them.

Enoch: Yes, again – everyone is ungrateful in his eyes.

TCG: Still, there is something important for us to know: *"On this side Jordan, in the land of Moab, began Moses* (are) *to declare this law, saying."* (Deuteronomy 1, 5) This essentially means that God had spoken and I, Moses, interpreted what he said.

Enoch: And what did he interpret?

TCG: We will find out in Deuteronomy 5: an interpretation of the Ten Commandments given to the Israelites by God.

Enoch: Really? I'm surprised to hear that.

The Second Message – Moses Accuses everyone

Enoch: I have noticed that Moses goes through all highlights of his life and summarizes everything he had down.

TCG: He speaks as if these were God's words again, giving a fiery speech about the past and the future of the Israelites. Everything which was promises to the forefathers would come to be and Moses speaks of his interpretation <u>and not God's</u>. It is not about right or wrong, but how Moses decided to accuse the people of everything which has happened to them, and not accounting for anything himself.

Enoch: Is it possible that he may have gone overboard with this?

TCG: He spoke about things that never happened, to draw the fire away from him and these issues are <u>critical for understanding</u>.

Enoch: What did he say?

TCG: Moses spoke highly of himself, speaking about how he stood alone in the face of danger and that all punishments inflicted upon the Israelites were out of their own doing: *"Send thou men, that they may search* ("Search", not "Spy") *the land of Canaan, which I give unto the children of Israel: of every tribe of their fathers shall ye send a man, every one a ruler among them."* (Numbers 13, 2) Is it conceivable that a "ruler "(chieftain) would be a spy?

Enoch: And Moses didn't send spies to search?

TCG: You tell me: *"And Moses sent them to spy out the land of Canaan, and said unto them, Get you up this way southward, and go up into the mountain: And see the land, what it is, and the people that dwelleth therein, whether they be strong or weak, few or many; And what the land is that they dwell in, whether it be good or bad; and what cities they be that they dwell in, whether in tents, or in strong holds."* (Numbers 13, 17-19) Moses wanted the spies to decide what exactly to do, not just report what they've seen.

Enoch: Is that a trap for the spies?

TCG: It appears so.

Enoch: What for? What would he have accomplished by doing so?

TCG: *"And they returned from searching of the land after forty days. And they went and came to Moses, and to Aaron, and to all the congregation of the children of Israel, unto the wilderness of Paran, to Kadesh; and brought back word unto them, and unto all the congregation, and shewed them the fruit of the land."* (Numbers 13, 25-26) Spies debrief their handler in private, why would they show their findings to everyone? Doesn't it seem like a trap to you? Moses was ordered to "search the land", as in like a tourist; he sent these men to spy – how is it that they are to blame for anything? Shouldn't they have analyzed their findings and only report them as they saw fit, in the eyes (and ears) of their handler only?

Enoch: So why would God be mad then?

TCG: Because God didn't mean for them to spy; he used this situation to punish these people of slaves by not entering The Promised Land.

Enoch: Shouldn't Moses be even a tiny-bit response for what has happened?

TCG: You can see for yourself that Moses was not willing to take any responsibility for their action. He lies deliberately and says so to the Israelites in Deuteronomy: *"And ye came near unto me every one of you, and said, We will send men before us, and they shall search us out the land, and bring us word again by what way we must go up, and into what cities we shall come. And the saying pleased me well: and I took twelve men of you, one of a tribe: And they turned and went up into the mountain, and came unto the valley of Eshcol, and searched it out. And they took of the fruit of the land in their hands, and brought it down unto* *us, and brought us word again, and said, It is a good land which the* LORD *our God doth give us."* (Deuteronomy 1, 22-25) So <u>Moses admitted that he was the one to send spies forward</u>, but removes himself from the equation by blaming the people for the action.

Enoch: Why was he trying to change the reality then?

TCG: Because of his egotistical character; he is on God's Side, the one passing judgement and the people? Guilty for their actions while Moses is innocent.

Enoch: That's low and selfish – is that a leader for a people?

TCG: Politics 101 – did you hear of any sole-ruler with accountability lately, hmm?

Enoch: But this is Moses, the prophet and saviour of the Israelites. Shouldn't he have tried to be responsible for what has happened to them?

TCG: This was probably his way of redeeming himself in the eyes of The Lord. Maybe this is how he'd get his ticket for entering Canaan after all and for God to absolve his sins...?

Enoch: Haha, so God will show him the way.

TCG: This is what Moses said unto the people then: *"And the* LORD *heard the voice of your words, and was wroth, and sware, saying, Surely there shall not one of these men of this evil generation see that good land, which I sware to give unto your fathers."* (Deuteronomy 1, 34-35) So Moses put God in the picture and took all the blame away from himself in the process.

Enoch: So he was saying that the reason he, Moses, was not part of the people to enter the land is due to the people? Ridiculous, what an outright lie right there!

TCG: You see, Enoch, leaders can say whatever they want to seem as if they were right.

Enoch: Moses was not worthy of actually entering Canaan, such an insidious individual.

TCG: He was no more different than any other contemporary leader.

Enoch: Fine, but badmouthing everyone? Disgusting.

The Third Message – Testaments of God

TCG: Enoch, you have become more bitter than ever.

Enoch: It hurts me: Moses was old and weary and now blamed his people for the injustice done unto him just so he might carry God's favour?

TCG: Do you think **that** would help him? Moses appears to be even "more human" than we first anticipated of him: God had shown him the land, he now knows what it is like to be so close yet so far. "Are all his efforts for nothing? " That is how he saw it. That is what you must understand.

Enoch: It's understanable, but why would God show him the Land of Canaan and then tell him he was not permitted to enter it? Just in spite?

TCG: Yes, one might understand it that way, but that was not God's intention. God had asked Moses to depart from the Promised Land; Moses finally realized that it was his time to go and the Israelites are now able and independent enough to continue without his guidance.

Enoch: I guess he didn't understand it this way, hence his bitterness.

TCG: But this message is beyond just that, you will see.

Enoch: What is it about then?

TCG: About keeping promises; whoever promises must be "reliable" and keep one's promises and testaments which were done.

Enoch: And who is this "reliable" person?

TCG: God, of course. That is why Moses was telling us, the readers, about God's plans of conquering the Land of Canaan as we appeared to be unable to understand the way God operates and what it is expected of us to do.

Enoch: What are you implying?

TCG: We are about to delve into the "infrastructure" of God's testaments and promises to Man.

Enoch: We have never delved into that before.

TCG: It's time. Listen, Enoch, the First Testament was done between God and Noah; this testament was done between God and humankind as to promise that God would never rain again and exterminate humanity. Do you remember now? In this testament, God "had realized" or even "made an excuse" by saying that "*for the imagination of man's heart is evil from his youth.*" (Genesis 8, 21) This is exactly how God saw it later on.

Enoch: So God says that it is of no use to exterminate humanity for evil or mischief of individuals or even whole groups.

TCG: Precisely; but we would delve into that a tad later when we are needed to.

The Second Testament was between God and Abraham and his seed, as he had promised Canaan to him and his progeny.

The Third (and last) Testament was between God and Jacob (Israel), as well as his progeny – the Israelites.

Enoch: I noticed that these circles are becoming smaller and smaller as we go, and these testaments are left between God and the Israelites solely, giving the entirety of the Land of Canaan to them.

TCG: So you think God didn't keep his other promises and testaments?

Enoch: What do you mean?

TCG: The testament he made with Abraham was relevant for Ismael, Esau, not to mention Lot's family (the Moabites and Ammonites); don't forget that they all descended from a common ancestor, the Aramites.

Enoch: So what are you saying, the other sons of Abraham and Isaac had a legitimate claim to the land as well? That is a political statement!

TCG: God has made his pact with the descendents of Abraham, even though he preferred focusing on the Israelites.

Enoch: How can you even make such a statement?

TCG: So it was written and decreed by Moses to the Israelites: *"And command thou the people, saying, Ye are to pass through the coast of your brethren the children of Esau...Meddle not with them; for I will not give you of their land, no, not so much as a foot breadth; because I have given mount Seir unto Esau for a possession."* (Deuteronomy 2, 4-5) Not enough? What do you think of this: *"And the LORD said unto me, Distress not the Moabites...for I will not give thee of their land for a possession; because I have given Ar unto the children of Lot for a possession...And when thou comest nigh over against the children of Ammon, distress them not...for I will not give thee of the land of the children of Ammon...because I have given it unto the children of Lot for a possession."* (Deuteronomy 2, 9-19)

Enoch: That is fantastic! I had no idea – I thought everything was promised to the Israelites.

TCG: The more we delve, the more it is implied that God had prior obligations as well and that he has no abandoned the other progeny of Abraham or his next of kin (Lot was Abraham's nephew).

Enoch: Thank you for this lesson in humility.

The Fourth Message – No Clemency

Enoch: I was thinking about the keeping of promises to the progeny of Abraham: indeed, God did not let the Israelites harm them, but he did not help them as promises to the Israelites, am I right?

TCG: Yes, it is even written so: *"In the same day the LORD made a covenant with Abram, saying, Unto thy seed have I given this land…The Kenites, and the Kenizzites, and the Kadmonites, And the Hittites, and the Perizzites, and the Rephaims, And the Amorites, and the Canaanites, and the Girgashites, and the Jebusites."* (Genesis 15, 18-21) Do you remember these?

Enoch: Yes, but I am asking how did God help them, as you said the Esauites were part of the covenant between God and Abraham, do you know the answer or do you assume to know it?

TCG: It is written how God had actively helped them.

Enoch: Where?

TCG: As it was written, the Land of Rephaims was given unto the Esauites: *"The Emims dwelt therein…a people great, and many, and tall, as the Anakims; Which also were accounted giants, as the Anakims; but the Moabites called them Emims. The Horims also dwelt in Seir beforetime; but the children of Esau succeeded them…and dwelt in their stead; as Israel did unto the land of his possession, which the LORD gave unto them."* (Deuteronomy 2, 10-12)

Enoch: I had no idea…

TCG: Did you notice the comparison between the Israelites and Esauites?

Enoch: Yes, but what does that tell us?

TCG: God said that the Esauites got their share, same as the Israelites got Canaan.

Enoch: I see that...odd, I did not realize that I indeed <u>did not realize that</u>.

TCG: Let's delve a little deeper, shall we Enoch? Let us understand the book better and see how God's promise comes to be.

Enoch: But this is a metaphor.

TCG: Is it? "*In the same day the LORD made a covenant with Abram, saying, Unto thy seed have I given this land, from the river of Egypt unto the great river, the river Euphrates.*" (Genesis 15, 18) Do you **now** understand the promise, Enoch?

Enoch: Yes, but...

TCG: People had never <u>fully understand the promise</u>. If we were to take Abraham's family and progeny (including Ismael, Esau, Isaac and Jacob), we would understand that the Arabs now living in Jordan are the progeny of Esau.

Enoch: But the Arabs had descended from Ismael, not Esau.

TCG: "*Then went Esau unto Ishmael, and took unto the wives which he had Mahalath the daughter of Ishmael Abraham's son, the sister of Nebajoth, to be his wife.*" (Genesis 28, 9)

Enoch: Yes, you are right – so it is true that the sons of Abraham dwell between the Euphrates and Egypt (and more) – I am shocked by this revelation. That is exactly what God had promised unto Abraham.

TCG: Do you see now, how people are unable to read thoroughly through The Book or that people's reading is solely based on selective understanding, not to mention nationalistic?

Enoch: Agreed.

TCG: The Israelites do have a mission to conquer "everything else", but in guile. How? By sending messengers to Sihon, king of Heshbon and ask to pass through his land peacefully. This is how the messengers spoke unto Sihon: *"Let me pass through thy land: I will go along by the high way, I will neither turn unto the right hand nor to the left...only I will pass through on my feet; (As the children of Esau which dwell in Seir, and the Moabites which dwell in Ar, did unto me;) until I shall pass over Jordan into the land which the LORD our God giveth us."* (Deuteronomy 2, 27-29)

Enoch: Sounded sincere to me. But would Sihon have had accommodated them?

TCG: *"But Sihon king of Heshbon would not let us pass by him: for the LORD thy God hardened his spirit, and made his heart obstinate, that he might deliver him into thy hand, as appeareth this day."* (Deuteronomy 2, 30) Do you now remember this trick?

Enoch: That's what God did to Pharaoh – the same trick to obliterate Egypt, the cunning of God and not for the first time.

TCG: Yes, one may see it that way but this ruse was to help the Israelites keep their "casualties" to the minimum as *"For by wise counsel thou shalt make thy war."* (Proverbs 24, 6)

Enoch: I cannot say that I am shocked, as we know God could be cruel to other people, as well as his people – the Israelites but there is a principle problem here.

TCG: Which is?

Enoch: Free will. If God takes it upon himself and doesn't leave Man with choice, what is the point of it all?

TCG: By swaying Sihon from letting the Israelites venture through his land?

Enoch: Yes, the point is that he did not hide it and told us publically that he had done so; that's very conceding of him to do so and shows us exactly why he is superior to us.

TCG: Yes, but God is indeed superior to Man; <u>think of all these chapters as a lesson.</u> In this lesson, we learn that one should not provide clemency towards one's enemies, as eventually, one may be cruel toward one's friends.

The second thing you may take with you is that by ruse <u>and not by war,</u> advantages are gained. It is thus complicated to judge God's behaviour without understanding all the intricate needlepoint done.

Enoch: Which is?

TCG: How would God bring these people to Canaan with as few casualties as possible.

Enoch: I do understand that, but God is not a mortal like us and cannot be expected to act in the same way. That is, God is temperamental. What about everything he taught us about the free will of choosing Good over evil?

TCG: Yes, but aren't the Israelites more important than Sihon and his people?

Enoch: So this is the "Jus Belli Justi" (Just War Theory)?

TCG: Not entirely, but these are means to an end.

Enoch: It is a good lesson, but very hard to grasp.

The Fifth Message – Moses the Colour Commentator

Enoch: Moses the prophet tells everyone what was happening.

TCG: One may think so; God decrees and Moses obeys, simple as that.

Enoch: Moses' Point of View entirely.

TCG: After the battle with Sihon and his cities, which were all given to the Israelites, we learn more about the Land of the Bashan and its king, Og. Do you understand the common denominator of these all? Consider this for a moment: "*And the LORD said unto me, Fear him not: for I will deliver him, and all his people, and his land, into thy hand; and thou shalt do unto him as thou didst unto Sihon king of the Amorites, which dwelt at Heshbon. So the LORD our God delivered into our hands Og also, the king of Bashan, and all his people: and we smote him until none was left to him remaining. And we took all his cities at that time, there was not a city which we took not from them, threescore cities, all the region of Argob, the kingdom of Og in Bashan. All these cities were fenced with high walls, gates, and bars; beside unwalled towns a great many.*" (Deuteronomy 3, 2-5)

Enoch: Why was Moses telling the readers about this?

TCG: You do not understand?

Enoch: But this is war God had waged, not Moses – why would Moses be glorifying himself for this?

TCG: Yes, but all God had done was through Moses, so Moses had taken these winnings as he was the one to execute God's decree. Moses was glorifying The Lord – he spoke about the many cities God had governed, how better equipped the city-dwellers were, how strong their walls were and how God delivered these cities into Moses' (and the people's) hands.

Enoch: Yes, but look at the brutality of it all: "*And we utterly destroyed them, as we did unto Sihon king of Heshbon, utterly destroying the men, women, and children, of every city.*" (Deuteronomy 3, 6) The Scorched Earth Policy – only livestock was taken alive and valuables were looted.

TCG: You speak of the morality of war but is war moral?

Enoch: It irks me to know that this war was not waged more humanely, it appears that Moses was hiding behind God's decree and tried to make this genocide a legitimate practice of sorts.

TCG: What irks me more is your naivety; the people were decreed to take the Land of Canaan by force, exercising their divine right by God himself where The Lord was the one to deliver the enemies of the Israelites into their hands. Did you expect the Israelites to show clemency towards the wounded and prisoners?

Enoch: Exterminating them was the better choice?

TCG: This was an army (and people) in the march; they had no land. They could not just stop, built prison camps and hospitals. They could not allow remnants of these people to produce future pockets of resistance. The Israelites exercised their divine right for the land, and yes it may not have appeared moral in your eyes, but this <u>was common practice</u> back then.

Enoch: I was just pointing out the brutality of war.

TCG: Let's now focus on something entirely different – Moses was telling the readers that there were wars where God had delivered the kings and cities unto the Israelites.

Enoch: Yes? Moses had already told the reader that the enemies of Israel were delivered into their hands, you said it yourself –

TCG: You do not see anything missing here?

Enoch: I am not into guesswork.

TCG: Was Joshua the one leading the men to battle? Not at all, he had no significance to God nor to Moses. But...that does not mean he did not fight, but he was not the one leading the men into battle. So Joshua meant nothing to Moses? It appears So.

Enoch: What are you implying?

TCG: As long as God needed Moses to be his messenger, Joshua had no part in these decisions – not God's nor Moses'.

Enoch: And? Why would **you** care about that?

TCG: You do not seem to grasp the intricacy of this situation: Moses wanted to continue leading the people. He was ignoring God's decree that he was not to enter the Land of Canaan at all. He was convinced that God still needed him, as God was the one to decree Moses to wage war and conquer and even if it seemed immoral to him, he would still feel obliged to do so.

Enoch: Was he able to reverse God's decree?

TCG: You need to first understand the dynamics between Moses and Joshua: Joshua was Moses' servant. Moses could never look at Joshua as his replacement – he never offered him to God as such, God was the one to choose him as such.
Strategically speaking, Joshua was always there: he was the one to lead the men into war with the Amalekites; this is why Moses never called for Joshua

to fight, as Moses thought that he would be the one to please The Lord. He naively believed that he was spared his judgement or at least had it postponed, to some degree.

Enoch: I surmised that, but how is it different than the other times you had told me about it <u>over and over</u>?

TCG: You will see for yourself, as the question remains as so: did Moses transfer the power of The Book to Joshua?

Enoch: I see.

The Sixth Message – Moses keeps narrating everything

Enoch: Moses kept talking about his (and the Israelites') triumphs; that is how he may feel important as he was dividing the land between the different tribes of Israel.

TCG: You may even notice that at this point God was not intervening in Moses' decisions. He needed to let Moses feel good about himself as well as important: *"And I commanded you at that time, saying, The Lord your God hath given you this land to possess it...Until the Lord have given rest unto your brethren, as well as unto you, and until they also possess the land which the Lord your God hath given them beyond Jordan...And I commanded Joshua at that time, saying, Thine eyes have seen all that the Lord your God hath done unto these two kings: so shall the Lord do unto all the kingdoms whither thou passest."* (Deuteronomy 3, 18-21) This is what Moses said to Joshua.

Enoch: Wait...what?! Moses was talking to Joshua, not God?

TCG: Paraphrasing Isaac's blessing to Jacob: The voice was God's, the mouth speaking it was Moses'. Do you remember when I told you that Moses never saw Joshua as his replacement and Moses wanted to keep leading the people? Moses was just unable to accept the fact that Joshua was to replace him, and this is why he was so adamant about leading.

Enoch: So Moses refused to step off?

TCG: Not in such, he kept offering his services to the people and God: *"And I besought the Lord at that time, saying, O Lord God, thou hast begun to shew thy servant thy greatness, and thy mighty hand...I pray thee, let me go over, and see the good land that is beyond Jordan...But the Lord was wroth with me for your sakes, and would not hear me...But charge Joshua, and encourage him, and strengthen him: for he shall go over before this people, and he shall cause them to inherit the land* *which thou shalt see."* (Deuteronomy 3, 23-28) Moses tried telling The Lord to spare him and allow him to cross the Jordan and see the land in his own eyes, but God could not have had been swayed from his decision. Moses was to see the land from a <u>mountain top and then die on it.</u>

Moses was no longer speaking to the readers, he was now decreed to make Joshua his successor in front of everyone. Did Moses want Joshua to succeed him though?

Enoch: It appeared not to be; the fact that there was a man like Joshua to interfere with Moses' plan of living and entering Canaan is so vivid.

TCG: It appeared that Moses thought Joshua unworthy to be his successor.

Enoch: What is your evidence for that?

TCG: Let us read between the lines, Moses is hardly even speaking to Joshua and does not even bother teaching him how to lead this nation. Joshua was a common man – he was chosen for his belief that God's way was the right way.

Enoch: Interesting; why was Caleb not the one to succeed Moses then? He was courageous and from the strongest of all the tribes – the Judah tribe. He was also the only spy to have said that the Land of Canaan was conquerable. Joshua even kept silent about that fact.

TCG: The answer is laid in front of you: Joshua was humble enough, which meant God would not have needed to persuade him as much as he would have had Caleb in turn. This was an advantage for God, as either way, God was to deliver the land into the hands of Joshua and all Joshua would have had to do was to obey.

Enoch: But why was Moses needed to die so far away from the land?

TCG: Once Moses dies, I will give you the reason for God's reason.

Enoch: This appears to be the third time in which God told Moses that he should go up the mountain and overlook the land from above before he died on it.

TCG: Moses was not emotionally ready to die yet. He still had that feeling that God may reverse or at least postpone his decree and that Moses was able to continue leading the people.

Enoch: I will accept that; what about Moses' decision to deliver The Book to Joshua?

TCG: I will speak about this later, I am unwilling to reveal the answer to that yet.

Enoch: Why?

TCG: It is not yet the time to reveal it. You are still unready to accept it. This is why you must walk this path in which I am leading you. In this way were God, Moses and Joshua going until they departed ways.

The Seventh Message – Take heed to yourselves

TCG: Well, did Moses receive his judgement willingly? Did he go up the mountain as he was told and die, Enoch?

Enoch: As far as I remember, Moses was never quick to go up – he is a slippery one.

TCG: You do not seem to think of him too much.

Enoch: I do not care for his behaviour towards the Israelites. He does not take responsibility as a leader should and blames them for all the misery which he brought unto them.

TCG: He brought unto them? They brought it unto them themselves.

Enoch: He was never clear about what was expected from them in The Book.

TCG: How could you even expect that from him? He was a novice at this, he was the prophet of Israel – for good or for worse.

Enoch: Perhaps so, but I am still mad at him for the "Sin of the Spies".

TCG: What?! The spies issue was a disaster!

Enoch: No arguments there, but <u>it was Moses</u> who sent spies instead of envoys to tour the land. He was the one who decided to send spies on a reconnaissance mission and sealed the fate of that generation to die in the desert.

TCG: Moses now sounds like God: *"Now therefore hearken, O Israel, unto the statutes and unto the judgments, which I teach you, for to do them, that ye may live, and go in and possess the land which the* Lord *God of your fathers giveth you."* (Deuteronomy 4, 1)

Enoch: I don't think I follow; God did not explain the laws already?

TCG: He did, but Moses would like to make them more meaningful by adding his interpretations to the mix: *"And Moses said unto the judges of Israel, Slay ye every one his men that were joined unto Baalpeor. And, behold, one of the children of Israel came and brought unto his brethren a Midianitish woman in the sight of Moses, and in the sight of all the congregation of the children of Israel...And when Phinehas, the son of Eleazar, the son of Aaron the priest, saw it, he rose up from among the congregation, and took a javelin...and thrust both of them through, the man of Israel, and the woman through her belly..." (Numbers 25, 5-8)* So Moses thinks that only the Levites (his own tribe) are the worthy ones to succeed him in this position, meaning that Phineas, his great-nephew, is the rightful heir.

Enoch: I remember that, why do you keep repeating this?

TCG: I told you there were clues aplenty as to who should succeed Moses.

Enoch: But it was already decided.

TCG: Moses conducted social engineering by speaking about the strong warrior who fought against the enemies of Israel.

Enoch: Phineas, but it was <u>a religious war</u>.

TCG: And who were the ones to slay the sinners worshipping the Golden Calf?

Enoch: The Levites, yes.

TCG: So what is your verdict?

Enoch: That Moses prefers a Levite as his replacement?

TCG: You tell me: *"Ye shall not add unto the word which I command you, neither shall ye diminish ought from it, that ye may keep the commandments of the LORD your God which I command you...for all the men that followed Baalpeor, the LORD thy God hath destroyed them from among you...Behold, I have taught you statutes and judgments, even as the LORD my God commanded me, that ye should do so in the land whither ye go to possess it. Keep therefore and do them; for this is your wisdom and your understanding in the sight of the nations, which shall hear all these statutes, and say, Surely this great nation is a wise and understanding people...And what nation is there so great, that hath statutes and judgments so righteous as all this law, which I set before you this day?"* (Deuteronomy 4, 2-8) Moses is implying that only the Levites were able to bring such victories to the Israelites and that the Israelites, in turn, were ungrateful towards them as only the Levites are fit to rule and the Israelites must listen to what God says if they are to even cross the Jordan and conquer Canaan.

The Eighth Message – Prophecies do come to pass

Enoch: I take it that Moses has accepted his fate and has now been telling the Israelites about what God had destined for him.

TCG: It appears so, but Moses still has a lot to "prophesy" and add his warnings for what is about to come.

Enoch: Prophesy? But he was the first prophet anyhow.

TCG: Let us delve into what he had to say to the Israelites: *"When thou shalt beget children...and shall corrupt yourselves, and make a graven image, or the likeness of any thing...that ye shall soon utterly perish from off the land whereunto ye go over Jordan to possess it; ye shall not prolong your days upon it...And the LORD shall scatter you among the nations, and ye shall be left few in number among the heathen, whither the LORD shall lead you."* (Deuteronomy 4, 25-27)

Enoch: It has a different meaning than I thought, I have never noticed that before.

TCG: You must always look into what is relevant, understand the warnings given. The Lord of Money (Mammon) is the replacement of the wooden and stone figurines: *"And there ye shall serve gods, the work of men's hands, wood and stone...But if from thence thou shalt seek the LORD thy God, thou shalt find him, if thou seek him with all thy heart and with all thy soul...even in the latter days, if thou turn to the LORD thy God, and shalt be obedient unto his voice."* (Deuteronomy 4, 28-30) This has already happened; this is how the State of Israel came to be in modern times.

Enoch: But does this end here?

TCG: Later on, but we already know what to look for and that is the lesson to be learnt for today.

Enoch: I see that he still focused on Baalpeor and how the Israelites won and conquered the land of the Moabites, but the Moabites also believed in the god which God warned the Israelites about and the Moabites were anxious to convert the Israelites therefore; so how come the Israelites did not annihilate them in the first place?

TCG: They were decreed to not touch the Moabites, have you forgotten?

Enoch: Because they were Esauites?

TCG: Precisely, as it was said in the Covenant of the pieces.

Enoch: So why not do the opposite: convert the Moabites to monotheism and believe in God instead of Baalpeor?

TCG: God had decided to focus solely on the Israelites, the sons of Jacob.

Enoch: Politics.

TCG: Maybe, but that is how God keeps his promises.

The Ninth Message – Can the people actually see?

TCG: Let us take a closer look at the clues given by Moses at the start of the Book of Deuteronomy. You see, Enoch, The Book of Deuteronomy is Moses' version after spending forty years in the desert, which started at the last month of that year from which Moses' tried to influence the people's decision and he had only 30 days to make it happen. God already wished for him to pass on beyond, so Moses allowed himself to say everything which was on his mind.

Enoch: So he has accepted his fate and accuses the Israelites of God's judgement of him.

TCG: Pretty much, yes: *"These be the words which Moses spake unto all Israel on this side Jordan in the wilderness... On this side Jordan, in the land of Moab, began Moses to declare this law, saying."* (Deuteronomy 1, 1-5) Moses had spoken to the people about all the laws that they must follow, to not wander the desert without guidance.

Enoch: Is that what you think he was doing?

TCG: Of course. First, he told them what he was planning on doing. He was transparent enough to accuse his "disciples", the Israelites, for all the wrongdoings and hardships done unto them.

Enoch: Secondly, he accused them of all the suffering which they inflicted unto him as well.

TCG: However, he did teach them to heed to God's laws, keeping what God demands of them so they may not suffer his wrath as mentioned in Deuteronomy 5: *"And Moses called all Israel, and said unto them, Hear, O Israel, the statutes and judgments which I speak in your ears this day, that ye may learn them, and keep, and do them. The LORD our God made a covenant with us in Horeb. The LORD made not this covenant with our fathers, but with us, even us, who are all* *of us here alive this day. The LORD talked with you face to face in the mount out of the midst of the fire, (I stood between the LORD and you at that time, to shew you the word of the LORD: for ye were afraid by reason of the fire, and went not up into the mount;) saying."* (Deuteronomy 5, 1-5) Moses was talking about the Covenant in Horev 40 years prior; most of the people standing in front of him was not even born yet, which gives us the impression that he was trying to boost the magnitude of it all.

Enoch: And what could we make of this?

TCG: He was essentially telling the people that God had spoken unto them, but they never heard it as they were too scared to, but he, Moses, did in fact hear it.

Enoch: He was referring to what was written about the Ten Commandments in Exodus 20, yes?

TCG: Precisely. We now understand what was written in Exodus: *"And all the people saw the thunderings, and the lightnings, and the noise of the trumpet, and the mountain smoking."* (Exodus 20, 18) The Israelites heard the noises and knew that God was speaking to them through the fire, but they were too far away to hear or understand what was being said, hence why it is written that they "saw the voices" and Moses already knew that they heard nothing, knowing that they were too afraid to come close which is why Moses was the only one to hear God's word.

Enoch: How is it possible that he never told them?

TCG: That is why it was never understood why it was written as: *"And they said unto Moses, Speak thou with us, and we will hear: but let not God speak with us, lest we die."* (Exodus 20, 19) Now, <u>do you understand</u>, Enoch, why God had told the people what he told the people?

Enoch: Let us simplify – they **did not know** the Ten Commandments?

TCG: Only vaguely, as they only knew what Moses had told them but they never heard what God had spoken.

Enoch: It appears we barely know what actually happened there.

The Tenth Message – The Ten Commandments

Enoch: So you are saying that the people <u>never enquired into</u> what God had spoken unto them?

TCG: They did, receiving what Moses wanted to pass unto them, but he did not have ample time to digest what God required of them. Moses needed to simplify the rules, so everyone may follow. The people never heard what was said, which is why Moses needed time "to translate" what was to be said to them.

Enoch: There are different versions, I remember you already mentioned that.

TCG: Let us understand what was written in The Book: in most versions of The Commandments, they are but a carbon copy of the original, which means that Moses received them as they were. The First and Second Commandments are about "the hierarchy" between God and Man and that Man has to worship God as to Man obligation to God for what God had done unto him (delivering Man from Egypt). The Second one speaks about monotheism and against any idolatry which may arise anywhere and everywhere, threatening with a vengeance should that ever take place.

Enoch: I have noticed that God doesn't force Man to believe in him, but that Man is not allowed to worship other gods.

TCG: Very true, the "freedom of choice" with the everlasting warning that it was God who delivered Israel from bondage in Egypt.

The Third one talks about not taking The Lord's name in vain, as this implies that God has responsibility for lies which had never taken place.

Enoch: And now about the Sabbath.

TCG: Yes, the "Achilles Heel" of the Ten Commandments.

Enoch: I do not understand why; these appear to be very logical.

TCG: Maybe so, but logic is not sufficient for people who wish to maximise their profits, even then money was most people's "God". So, how would one prevent others from working on the Sabbath, to understand that it was for their own good?

Enoch: A ruse?

TCG: Moses had understood that the law's purpose was for the betterment of Man, where the law and teachings become a living trait of social justice for anyone who lives, without taking into account their status, not working on the seventh day – Man as well as animal. The Sabbath is for the whole world, where work stops even for a brief moment. But how would you make people do this? By making the Sabbath a holy day, which belongs to God. When God spoke on Mount Sinai, he said: *"For in six days the LORD made heaven and earth, the sea, and all that in them is, and rested the seventh day: wherefore the LORD blessed the sabbath day, and hallowed it."* (Exodus 20, 11) Sufficient enough for you, Enoch?

Enoch: It appears so, yes.

TCG: It appears to me that Moses was a reasonable man here; why would Man care that God worked six days and rested on the seventh? I am telling you, Man never cared for that.

Enoch: So why?

TCG: Moses thought it over and used the same sentence for the First Commandment; we will get to that soon enough, but let us see what Moses says about the Sabbath and how could one interpret it as it was more important than all the others combined, which is why he revised and added on it.

Enoch: "Revised"? Did its meaning change then?

TCG: No, but it was made "clearer". What did God intend by keeping the Sabbath? Who was it for?

Remember that God speaks succinctly: *"But the seventh day is the sabbath of the* L ORD *thy God: in it thou shalt not do any work, thou, nor thy son, nor thy daughter, thy manservant, nor thy maidservant, nor thy cattle, nor thy stranger that is within thy gates."* (Exodus 20, 10) Moses understood that God meant that Man should not be working on the Sabbath, but how would that come to be in practice: *"But the seventh day is the sabbath of the* L ORD *thy God: in it thou shalt not do any work, thou, nor thy son, nor thy daughter, nor thy manservant, nor thy maidservant, nor thine ox, nor thine ass, nor any of thy cattle...And remember that thou wast a servant in the land of Egypt, and that the* L ORD *thy God brought thee out thence through a mighty hand and by a stretched out arm: therefore the* L ORD *thy God commanded thee to keep the sabbath day."* (Deuteronomy 5, 14-15) So because Man was a slave in Egypt and was delivered by God from bondage, then you, Man, should keep the Sabbath and not even allow your servants to work on it. These are the first civil rights granted to Man.

Enoch: Pretty clear; so no living creature is allowed to work on the Sabbath. But why would animals not work on the Sabbath?

TCG: They too have rights.

Enoch: So what is Sabbath to God? That Man must rest and not labour and earn money and not even think of working? People should not do what they must for their home? And what about the rest of the Ten Commandments?

TCG: These have not been revised and stayed the same as they were in Exodus.

Enoch: But for the Israelites that have not heard them from day one, these are the only ones that matter.

TCG: The fact that God did not intervene tells us a multitude about his approval of them.

Enoch: May I have a summary of what the Sabbath was for the Israelites?

TCG: No work and only rest for everyone, every living creature and why? Because when the Israelites were slaves in Egypt, they were not allowed to rest at all and that is inhuman to do so unto others.

Enoch: And the wife? Why was she excluded from this?

TCG: I do not think I follow your logic.

Enoch: *"in it thou shalt not do any work, thou, nor thy son, nor thy daughter, nor thy manservant, nor thy maidservant, nor thine ox, nor thine ass, nor any of thy cattle, nor thy stranger that is within thy gates; that thy manservant and thy maidservant may rest as well as thou."* I do not see the wife in this.

TCG: Do you know that no one has ever asked this before?

Enoch: Neither did God mention her nor Moses paid it heed. Any reason for that?

TCG: Let me confer and get back to about this.

The Eleventh Message – The Wife is Excluded

TCG: I have returned to you with an answer; it is a rather tricky one for gender-equality supporters. It is said that one should work for six days, <u>doing all of one's labour</u>. That is the decree.

Enoch: So work is a decree, not a necessity?

TCG: If it had no importance, God would have implied that Man could do whatever Man pleases for six days, while the seventh is holy. So, Man must work for six days but that work does not have to be a physical one. Having said that, the word "labour" does appear, thus we must understand why the wife had been excluded from this decree.

Enoch: Which is? You are confusing me.

TCG: God <u>did not say</u> that one should not labour, but one should not do **one's labour**. Which means that if it is your day-job, you cannot do it on the Sabbath.

Enoch: So one could work as long as it is not one's day-job?

TCG: Precisley; one cannot work in a job which would provide one with profit, but if for example a painting fell or if the roof is leaking, one could mend it.

Enoch: And the wife?

TCG: The wife was excluded as most women back then were <u>housewives</u>, that is women needed to cook, feed, take care of the livestock, milk the goats, cows, whichever and clean. Livestock <u>must be milked</u> everyday, including on the Sabbath and they must eat as well.

Enoch: So, if I understand you correctly, the "labour" which is mentioned to be forbidden on the Sabbath is not forbidden for the wife, as she is the centre and pivot-point of the house.

TCG: Exactly; let us become philosophical for a moment: God had worked six days that week and rested on the Sabbath – does it sound logical to you that <u>he was not maintaining</u> the world during that time? But, the point of this decree was to allow people a resting day in which they do not have to work.

Enoch: But the wife is excluded from this decree as no one gives a damn?

TCG: On the contrary; no one can observe the Sabbath <u>without the wife taking care of everything</u>. Now do you understand the wife's importance? She too understands that this job must be maintained.

Enoch: Now I understand why everyone else was mentioned but the wife in that decree.

TCG: When I was presented with this resolution, Enoch, I understood why Moses did not ask God how come the wife was excluded. I realized also <u>that he was not asked about it</u> by the people either, as it was as clear as day for everyone.

The Twelfth Message – Honour thy father and thy mother

Enoch: I find it hard to fathom the fact that the wife was excluded.

TCG: I understand that this equality disequilibirium is difficult for you, but the wife did understand it well enough as this was her job, but let us move on to move novelties from our prophet Moses.

Enoch: Such as?

TCG: *"a great voice: and he added no more. And he wrote them in two tables of stone, and delivered them unto me."* (Deuteronomy 5, 22) this is what Moses had added once he finished reading The Tablets to the Israelites; he has added everything else that he felt was necessary for the Israelites. But God gave Moses only the words which were on the tablets, the commandments solely – without any interpretation.

Enoch: I understand that.

TCG: Do you?

God had given The Commandments on the tablets, that is all – he never asked for interpretations, nor did he offer any in return. Everything else was Moses' idea, as the people were too afraid to come forth next to the mountain and hear God's words unto them, asking Moses to be their delegate: *"Go thou near, and hear all that the LORD our God shall say: and speak thou unto us all that the LORD our God shall speak unto thee; and we will hear it, and do it. And the LORD heard the voice of your words, when ye spake unto me; and the LORD said unto me, I have heard the voice of the words of this people, which they have spoken unto thee: they have well said all that they have spoken."* (Deuteronomy 5, 27-28)

Enoch: Fine, but what did Moses teach the people then?

TCG: Everything which God decrees must be obeyed, you and your son and grandson and whomever in your family, so you may live longer.

Enoch: Such as: *"Honour thy father and thy mother, as the LORD thy God hath commanded thee; that thy days may be prolonged, and that it may go well with thee, in the land which the LORD thy God giveth thee."* (Deuteronomy 5, 16)

TCG: And what do you make of this? God is the Israelites mother and father, and they must obey because they understand that is the right way in which they must follow. This is why you understand why it was then told to them that if they do so, their "days may be prolonged, and that it may go well with thee, in the land..."

The Thirteenth Message – Who is the real servant?

Enoch: Moses to me is like Scheherazade in One Thousand and One Nights.

TCG: I will giggle at that, but tell me more.

Enoch: Moses knows that he was about to die.

TCG: He was <u>destined to die</u> but only when God has decided so, for now he was only preparing Moses for it. Moses was still very much interested for the people to believe in God: *"And thou shalt love the* L*ord thy God with all thine heart...And these words, which I command thee this day, shall be in thine heart: And thou shalt teach them diligently unto thy children...And thou shalt bind them for a sign upon thine hand, and they shall be as frontlets between thine eyes."* (Deuteronomy 6, 5-8) So Man must love God with all of Man's heart and might. Can you imagine of such love at all times <u>in every waking moment</u> and for everyone to see how you express this love?

Enoch: But why must this love be forced? Why must it be so intense? The people should want to express this love unto God, not be forced to do so.

TCG: That is the beauty of expressing one's love towards one's God.

Enoch: You cannot force love on someone. This reminds me of the fable of the Hebrew Servant: *"if thou buy an Hebrew servant, six years he shall serve: and in the seventh he shall go out free for nothing. If he came in by himself...if he were married, then his wife shall go out with him...And if the servant shall plainly say, I love my master, my wife, and my children; I will not go out free: Then his master shall bring him unto the judges; he shall also bring him to the door, or unto the door post; and his master shall bore his ear through with an aul; and he shall serve him for ever."* (Exodus 21, 2-6) He would be branded as for the love of his master and God?

TCG: What are you implying?

Enoch: Man is servant to God and I'll explain as it was so written: it Moses was his God's servant and Joshua was his own servant (Moses'), so what was Joshua? And if the people are being led by a servant or the servant's servant (in the KJV version, Joshua is mentioned as Moses' minister), what is the people? A people of slaves.

TCG: I do not see how you could compare between the servant who said he loved his master and the Hebrew who puts on a piece of leather on his hands saying that he loves his master – is that the same thing?

Enoch: And on his forward and on his house's posts, on the gates, everywhere for that matter. Same thing.

TCG: I am appalled by the comparison, but there is some merit in what you are saying. It is peculiar in my eyes though that you were able to entwine these two together and consider them similar in the notion of "love".

Enoch: And what is the difference between the semantics of the servant who calls his master "my lord" and Man who calls his God "My Lord"?

TCG: Man is not a servant of God.

Enoch: Why not? Is it extreme to think that way?

TCG: Moses was God's messenger to the people, who in fact was a servant of God as he had to deliver God's word unto the people.

Does it make sense for you now?

Enoch: I will accept this etymology, yes.

The Fourteenth Message – Why was Moses let go?

Enoch: I must confess to something.

TCG: Which is?

Enoch: I do not know which side you are on and who sent you this way. Moreover, I am not sure if you are telling me your version of the story or if that is the dogma/

TCG: *"But as for thee, stand thou here by me, and I will speak unto thee all the commandments, and the statutes, and the judgments, which thou shalt teach them..."* (Deuteronomy 5, 31) This is what Moses told the Israelites after reading them the Ten Commandments.

Enoch: So he was essentially speaking God's words as if they were colleagues of sorts?

TCG: That act had given Moses the legitimacy to pass unto Man the laws of The Lord. Moses' plan was to glorify God in a last attempt of clemency from God, a moment before entering Canaan. He thought that had he done so unto the people, God would pardon him and let him in as well.

Enoch: So what was the problem?

TCG: *"Now these are the commandments, the statutes, and the judgments, which the LORD your God commanded to teach you, that ye might do them in the land whither ye go to possess it: That thou mightest fear the LORD thy God, to keep all his statutes and his commandments, which I command thee, thou, and thy son...Hear therefore, O Israel, and observe to do it; that it may be well with thee, and that ye may increase mightily, as the LORD God of thy fathers hath promised thee, in the land that floweth with milk and honey...And thou shalt love the LORD thy God with all thine heart, and with all thy soul, and with all thy might. And these words, which I command thee this day, shall be in thine heart: And thou shalt teach them diligently unto thy children...And thou shalt bind them for a sign upon thine hand, and they* *shall be as frontlets between thine eyes...And it shall be, when the LORD thy God shall have brought thee into the land which he sware unto thy fathers, to Abraham, to Isaac, and to Jacob, to give thee great and goodly cities...when thou shalt have eaten and be full."* (Deuteronomy 6, 1-11) So the Israelites would receive everything they wanted but they were warned also that they must obey The Lord.

Enoch: So Moses promised that God would not have to make a lot of effort and would receive everything from The Lord as long as Man keeps God's decree and heed to God's warnings; not too complicated.

TCG: Yes, Moses was thus understood by the Israelites and it was mentioned in his introduction that he was speaking God's words.

Enoch: It was a little extreme, but that is definitely a very nice promise to the people.

TCG: And for this Man would receive all this bounty: *"Thou shalt fear the LORD thy God, and serve him, and shalt swear by his name. Ye shall not go after other gods, of the gods of the people which are round about you; (For the LORD thy God is a jealous God among you) lest the anger of the LORD thy God be kindled against thee, and destroy thee from off the face of the earth."* (Deuteronmy 6, 13-15) This was a promise, not a suggestion. Moses promises in the name of The Lord but even had he was able to keep these promises, they would never happen.

Enoch: Why? Were the Israelites not promises these miracles?

TCG: They were, but by Moses <u>not God.</u>

Enoch: So Moses lied?

TCG: No, he too believed these fairytales. He too did not know how difficult the Israelites' lives would be, conquering the land.

Enoch: So what are you saying?

TCG: That Moses must die. He cannot find a place in this brave new world. He needs to be replaced with someone a lot more "practical".

Enoch: Someone who realizes how the world works.

TCG: Yes. Less miracles and more faith in the way and that the land was promised to the Israelites.

Enoch: And Moses cannot be taught this?

TCG: Not so much; he cannot see God as a "failing" one. In his eyes, God is everything. Moses was alone in the world without a wife or progeny – what else was he left with?

Enoch: Yes, he did leave his wife and children behind. What else was he left with, his "career", hehe.

TCG: But he loved the "roughtneck" people. They are "his children" and he felt responsible and obliged to them. In his eyes, his calling has never ended.

The Fifteenth Message – Writing cheques he cannot cover

Enoch: I see that Moses keeps describing what might happen to the ones not abiding by God's decrees. Moses explicitly mentioned this: "*And when thy son asketh thee in time to come, saying, What mean the testimonies, and the statutes, and the judgments, which the LORD our God hath commanded you? Then thou shalt say unto thy son, We were Pharaoh's bondmen in Egypt; and the LORD brought us out of Egypt with a mighty hand.*" (Deuteronomy 6, 20-21)

TCG: God is entitled to whichever he wishes on account of what he had done unto the Israelites' forefathers. Everything is pretty much summed up in this passage: "*and the LORD commanded us to do all these statutes, to fear the LORD our God, for our good always, that he might preserve us alive, as it is at this day.*" (Deuteronomy 6, 24) Moses was trying hard to make sure the people loved, respected and adhered to God's decree, so they may indeed prosper in Canaan once they reached it.

Enoch: Indeed as it was written about Scheherazade: As long as she kept telling the Sultan magnificent stories, he spared her life. As such, Moses believed that had he kept complimenting God whenever possible, perhaps God would, in turn, grant him mercy and naturally, the people would believe that all these hardships were not in vain.

TCG: The hope that God would grant Moses clemency keeps Moses' spirit up, which leads us to the next passage which tells the Israelites all that they must know: "*Wherefore it shall come to pass, if ye hearken to these judgments, and keep, and do them, that the LORD thy God shall keep unto thee the covenant and the mercy which he sware unto thy fathers: And he will love thee, and bless thee, and multiply thee: he will also bless the fruit of thy womb, and the fruit of thy land, thy corn, and thy wine, and thine oil, the increase of thy kine, and the flocks of thy sheep, in the land which he sware unto thy fathers to give thee.*" (Deuteronomy 7, 12-13)

Enoch: No more than empty promises, how could he even promise them such a thing? An idyll which exists in fairytales.

TCG: Now you understand why Moses must go. He has done his bidding, but he has promised things that would never happen. Moses believed his own lies; he saw the Promised Land as the "Lost Paradise" (Garden of Eden) to which the Israelites would return.

Enoch: Does he not understand that the Israelites would just be another people in Canaan?

TCG: He is unable to grasp it. He thought that suffering for 40 years in the desert with these "roughneck people" and a jealous God constituted the end of this chapter. He did not understand that the journey of the Israelites did not finish there and that he, Moses, would not be the one leading them to victory.

Enoch: Old as he was, wise as he was, naïve he remained.

TCG: More a "devout man" than anything else. He believed in justice and just judgement, doing good. But arriving in Canaan was but a wake-up call for Moses. In this reality, Joshua could not endure and succeed with Moses breathing down his neck, step-by-step, overseeing and trying to pull the strings. We also see in Chapter 9 that there is a reference to the spies and what happened afterwards. Do you remember how Moses treated the spies who were telling horror stories about the land?

Enoch: How could I forget? Because of it, the Israelites were wandering the desert for 40 years to make the entire generation perish as they were too afraid to enter the Land of Canaan.

TCG: Let us see how the truth is then told: *"Hear, O Israel: Thou art to pass over Jordan this day, to go in to possess nations greater and mightier than thyself, cities great and fenced up to heaven, A people great and tall, the children of the Anakims, whom thou knowest, and of whom thou hast heard say, Who can stand before the children of Anak[1] Understand therefore this day, that the LORD thy God is he which goeth over before thee; as a consuming fire he shall destroy them, and he shall bring them down before thy face: so shalt thou drive them out, and destroy them quickly, as the LORD hath said unto thee. "* (Deuteronomy 9, 1-3) So Moses repeated which was reported to him by the spies and then added his "soothing ointment", if you will – there may be giants, but God is on the Israelites' side and he shall consume these giants without even breaking a sweat.

Enoch: And to think what would have happened had Moses spoken that way 40 years back...

TCG: Yes, very true.

Enoch: I am sorry, but this sounds like God was looking for this to happen just so he could keep them in the desert.

TCG: You are faithless then in God, Enoch.

Enoch: No, just a realist.

---

[1] "Anak" is the Hebrew word for "giant". It is not known if this was a person's/people's name or a reference to the fact that they were giants.

The Sixteenth Message – Moses' Sacrifice

TCG: *"Speak not thou in thine heart, after that the LORD thy God hath cast them out from before thee, saying, For my righteousness the LORD hath brought me in to possess this land: but for the wickedness of these nations the LORD doth drive them out from before thee."* (Deuteronomy 9, 4)

Enoch: Unbelievable! Moses accused the people of being ungrateful, faithless and insincere, he blames everyone but himself.

TCG: Moses said that the Israelites are unworthy of Canaan for they were sinners, but the gentiles were even bigger ones.

Enoch: So God was doing the Israelites a favour by letting them inside Canaan? Why would they even consider doing so, knowing they were "unworthy of God's love"?

TCG: Moses was hurt; he believed that because of the Israelites, he was denied entry into Canaan, and after all, he had done for them. This is the rest of his tirade: *"Not for thy righteousness, or for the uprightness of thine heart, dost thou go to possess their land: but for the wickedness of these nations the LORD thy God doth drive them out from before thee, and that he may perform the word which the LORD sware unto thy fathers, Abraham, Isaac, and Jacob. Understand therefore, that the LORD thy God giveth thee not this good land to possess it for thy righteousness; for thou art a stiffnecked people."* (Deuteronomy 9, 5-6)

Enoch: What a "loving father" he was for the Israelites.

TCG: It is hard for you to see Moses like this; he was romanticised for centuries as a saviour, a miracle from God, a prophet – name your cliché. But in truth, Moses was just as human as you or anyone else for that matter and had his weaknesses.

Enoch: I cannot think of him this way; the Israelites trusted him and now they cannot go back to Egypt; they cannot stay in the desert either. He made them believe that he was the rightful leader, taking their lives in his hands and doing whatever he pleased with them in the desert. I, for one, believe that this has happened because he lost his authority among the people: Miriam died as well as Aharon, with all their privileges – Moses' family had no more power. This seems a simulated situation, not coincidental.

TCG: That is a grave accusation. Moses believed he was destined to venture into Canaan with them; he never expected to be taken away from them once they were on the brink of reaching Canaan.

Enoch: He implied that he was betrayed: <u>he twice fasted</u> after breaking The Tablets and after the Golden Calf Incident.

TCG: *"And the L*ORD *said unto me, Arise, get thee down quickly from hence; for thy people which thou hast brought forth out of Egypt have corrupted themselves; they are quickly turned aside out of the way which I commanded them; they have made them a molten image. Furthermore the L*ORD *spake unto me, saying, I have seen this people, and, behold, it is a stiffnecked people: Let me alone, that I may destroy them, and blot out their name from under heaven: and I will make of thee a nation mightier and greater than they."* (Deuteronomy 9, 12-14)

Enoch: So God acknowledged the fact that he was the one to deliver them from Egypt and states that he would annihilate this generation and <u>create a new people</u> from **their seed**?

TCG: You hit the nail on the head.

The Seventeenth Message – Moses' Epiphany

TCG: We now know how Moses had felt about the Golden Calf, but here's a revelation – did you know that God was contemplating killing Aaron?

Enoch: What?! How so?

TCG: *"And when the people saw that Moses delayed to come down out of the mount, the people gathered themselves together unto Aaron, and said unto him, Up, make us gods...And Aaron said unto them, Break off the golden earrings, which are in the ears of your wives...And all the people brake off the golden earrings which were in their ears, and brought them unto Aaron. And he received them at their hand, and fashioned it with a graving tool, after he had made it a molten calf: and they said, These be thy gods, O Israel, which brought thee up out of the land of Egypt."* (Exodus 32, 1-4) Yes, the Golden Calf was made by Aaron himself.

Enoch: I see, but how were they able to build this idol? How much gold could they possibly have had?

TCG: From the Egyptians: *"And the children of Israel did according to the word of Moses; and they borrowed of the Egyptians jewels of silver, and jewels of gold, and raiment: And the LORD gave the people favour in the sight of the Egyptians, so that they lent unto them such things as they required. And they spoiled the Egyptians."* (Exodus 12, 35-36)

Enoch: "Borrowed"...? A moment ago, the Egyptians were weeping over their dead firstborn, now they become the philanthropists?

TCG: Agreed, but why was it written like that then?

Enoch: So it would appear as if the Egyptians started believing in God as opposed to their own gods; and still, it makes no sense to me.

TCG: But <u>why is it written like that?</u> You were already given enough clues from me about this.

Enoch: A metaphor?

TCG: Exactly. I have told you more than once that what matters is not what had actually happened, but why was it brought to our attention. Everything is biased and appears to be written to favour one side over the other. This is what we are here for: to separate the wheat from the chaff.

Enoch: That is it? Critical thinking?

TCG: Let us review this: the Hebrews took jewellery from the Egyptians, so when they needed to build their Golden Calf, they had the raw materials for it close by.

Enoch: Fine, but who was asking for the Golden Calf to be moulded in the first place?

TCG: Everyone who had believed in the God of Israel as well as the "mixed multitude" (people of various ethnicities that left Egypt with the Israelites).

Enoch: How did you surmise that?

TCG: As only the multitude could have thought that a Golden Calf is the Hebrew God, who is known to be shapeless and invisible. Also notice that they have mentioned God is plural form "these be <u>thy gods</u>". Why would a monotheistic people consider their God to be a multitude of such? Meaning that they too did not believe in God.

Enoch: So how come Aaron was not struck immediately? Why was he spared?

TCG: He had Moses' grace. He was the one to send the Levites to kill all those who participated in the worshipping of The Calf, so we know that he did not harm Aaron. And now Moses even reminds the people not just about his sacrifice, but his brother's as well: *"And the LORD was very angry with Aaron to have destroyed him: and I prayed for Aaron also the same time."* (Deuteronomy 9, 20) That is naturally after saying to the people what they did wrong: *"Ye have been rebellious against the LORD from the day that I knew you."* (Deuteronomy 9, 23)

Enoch: How dare he accuse them?! Did he listen to everything given by God?

TCG: Did he not do what he was asked to do?

Enoch: He did not always do so. Moses told the people how they wronged God by listening to the spies and why they were punished and he was in turn punished for individual ministerial responsibility.

TCG: Is it so? Show me where it was written.

Enoch: When Moses was told to only speak to the rock for it to produce water and he hit it with his staff instead.

TCG: True.

Enoch: Moses was feeding the people "fake news", so he could save face while making them wander the desert for forty years; he knew no one would actually remember what has happened and no one would tell it to his face either that they were punished because of him.

TCG: Leaders are also human, I told you that before. These stories are metaphors and allegories which are there to explain something; look at them as sort of parables there to teach us, the readers, about what has happened and what was to be.

Consider this for a moment: if all the gold was molten to produce The Calf and everything was lost inside the belly of the earth as mentioned, how did the Israelites create the Tabernacle...?

Politicians lie; they just expect everyone else to forget their lies.

The Eighteenth Message – Moses' Side of the Story

Enoch: I find it hard to follow a leader who keeps lying and distorting reality.

TCG: This is how people tell apart between fiction and reality. In antiquity, leaders needed to defend themselves, being cunning and able to leverage any opportunity given to them. That is exactly the "Secret of the Bible".

Enoch: So there is no good? Only bad?

TCG: One cannot have good without bad, this is how the world works.

Enoch: One cannot teach others to be bad.

TCG: You are using a modern magnifying glass after years of Enlightenment about morals, rules and ethics to try and discover why the ancients acted the way they acted. This is not how it works.

Enoch: I do understand that once Moses realised he would not be permitted into Canaan, he became more "human" and started blaming the people for his political demise and losing favour in the eyes of The Lord, they do seem ungrateful in his eyes.

TCG: Do you believe that? Do you think that Moses was not the conniving type beforehand?

Enoch: I think this is the first time you told me about Moses "rigging"; he brought this on himself in front of the people.

TCG: And what is your point? Should "dirty laundry" always be washed in public?

Enoch: Yes, leaders should strive to be transparent – did Moses lie to the people before?

TCG: If you read the passages thoroughly, you would understand that there is barely an anomaly between how he was acting in Deuteronomy than how he was acting in Exodus, Leviticus and Numbers. This is a pattern, not progress.

Enoch: Explain.

TCG: Moses did, decided or reacted without ever consulting with God; in most cases, he was defying God's specific orders either in actions or in words.

Enoch: You are speaking in tongues again, you need to be more coherent.

TCG: *"And Moses sent messengers from Kadesh unto the king of Edom, Thus saith thy brother Israel, Thou knowest all the travail that hath befallen us: How our fathers went down into Egypt, and we have dwelt in Egypt a long time; and the Egyptians vexed us, and our fathers And when we cried unto the LORD, he heard our voice, and sent an angel, and hath brought us forth out of Egypt: and, behold, we are in Kadesh, a city in the uttermost of thy border: Let us pass, I pray thee, through thy country: we will not pass through the fields, or through the vineyards, neither will we drink of the water of the wells: we will go by the king's high way, we will not turn to the right hand nor to the left, until we have passed thy borders. And Edom said unto him, Thou shalt not pass by me, lest I come out against thee with the sword. And the children of Israel said unto him, We will go by the high way: and if I and my cattle drink of thy water, then I will pay for it: I will only, without doing anything else, go through on my feet."* (Numbers 20, 14-19) As you can see, Moses was not looking for trouble, sending emissaries asking to travel via the Edomite Kingdom. The King of Edom refused to do so, so a war broke out.

Enoch: So why did the Israelites not fight? Worried that God would not help them, despite his promise to their forefathers? Why did Moses not consult with God about how to attack the enemies of Israel? Why was Edom spared?

TCG: Moses never went to war with the Edomites; he went to Sihon, the king of the Amorites and asked for the same privileges; when Sihon refused, they went to war annihilating him and his entire kingdom in the process.

Enoch: Why would he do so then? I mean, fighting Sihon over fighting the Edomites prolonged the Israelites' journey into Canaan. What is going on here?

TCG: That is exactly what I am trying to convey to you – Moses' ambivalent and ambiguous nature. He was cooperating with God in prolonging the journey.

Enoch: Sounds peculiar to me.

TCG: Moses had forgotten that <u>he chose not to fight the Edomites</u> because the negotiations failed. A moment later, on the brink of entering Canaan, do we the readers understand why the King of the Edomites was referred to as "Brother" by Moses.

Enoch: Explain.

TCG: The Edomites were cousins to the Israelites; Esau, Jacob's (Israel) brother was the original leader of the Edomites and their forefather. Ismael (Abraham's son and Isaac's half-brother) married into Esau's Edomite as well, meaning that they were in fact brothers[2]: *"And command thou the people, saying, Ye are to pass through the coast of your brethren the children of Esau, which dwell in Seir; and they shall be afraid of you: take ye good heed unto yourselves therefore: Meddle not with them; for I will not give you of their land, no, not so much as a foot breadth; because I have given mount Seir unto Esau for a possession. Ye shall buy meat of them for money, that ye may eat; and ye shall also buy water of*

---

[2] "Brothers" was a reference to any next of kin in antiquity; cousins were considered brothers and so were nephews, as was customary among the Romans to adopt nephews as heirs and consider them "sons".

them for money, that ye may drink." (Deuteronomy 2, 4-6) The negotiation was futile as Moses was ordered not to fight the Edomite brethren of the Israelites.

Enoch: So why did Moses not mention that fact?

TCG: Ego. He could not have said that the Edomites are their brothers, hence they cannot fight them. The people needed to see victories and Moses delivered those to maintain his exercising of power over the people. He needed to appear strong in their eyes to maintain sovereignty.

The Nineteenth Message – Much ado about a (Golden) Calf

TCG: Let us try and understand the "clue" given to us here, the "metaphor", if you will.

Enoch: I agree; I think it is time we separated the wheat from the chaff.

TCG: Moses was still accusing the Israelites of everything they had all needed to endure: *"And I took your sin, the calf which ye had made, and burnt it with fire, and stamped it, and ground it very small, even until it was as small as dust: and I cast the dust thereof into the brook that descended out of the mount."* (Deuteronomy 9, 21)

Enoch: Again with the Golden Calf?

TCG: You are focusing on the wrong element; do you remember how the Israelites got the gold for the Calf to begin with, which was <u>sculptured by Aaron</u>?

Enoch: Earrings, rings, jewellery – no?

TCG: Since when do <u>slaves own jewellery</u>?

Enoch: They took it from the Egyptians, it says so.

TCG: With no incident? They just gave them their jewellery willingly? These people were mourning for their fallen firstborn: *"They have turned aside quickly out of the way which I commanded them: they have made them a molten calf, and have worshipped it, and have sacrificed thereunto, and said, These be thy gods, O Israel, which have brought thee up out of the land of Egypt."* (Exodus 32, 8)

Bear in mind here, Enoch, how God addresses the ones to initiate the sculpting of the Calf: "these be thy Gods, O Israel..." – **Gods** not <u>God</u>.

Enoch: Fine, then who are the ones who had so many jewellery?

TCG: The Mixed Multitude; many different people of different ethnicities who wanted to entwine their fates with the Israelites', and were accepted as such by Moses.

Enoch: How do you know how many of these were actually present within the Israelites' ranks?

TCG: Do you know how much gold would be needed for such a statue? These people had jewellery <u>because they were not slaves</u>. Moses was absent for six hours and they already used up the opportunity to convert the Israelites and who was to blame for this? The Israelites, naturally.

Enoch: I see.

TCG: But let us delve into this more and understand what was the Golden Calf incident all about. We understand that the Israelites were looking for a meaning behind the belief in God, which transcends the spiritual – they needed something tangible which they could worship, like everyone else around them. This is why you see The Scriptures in synagogues, churches and mosques – people need "to see" God.

Enoch: Well, what is the alternative to The Calf then?

TCG: The Tabernacle, the strong odour arising from the sacrifices given – reeducating the Israelites in God's will.

Enoch: So what? Moses should not have accused the Israelites, condemning them while he considers himself "righteous". What is a father for? He is not like Balam, cursing and cursing.

The Twentieth Message – Moses was not done yet (accusing)

TCG: Moses was not done accusing the Israelites, showing the error of their ways at every turn. Was he right for doing so, or was it possible that he was lying to the people, exploiting their weak memory?

Enoch: I too do not remember; would you refreshen mine?

TCG: *"And at Taberah, and at Massah, and at Kibrothhattaavah, ye provoked the LORD to wrath. Likewise when the LORD sent you from Kadeshbarnea...then ye rebelled against the commandment of the LORD your God, and ye believed him not, nor hearkened to his voice. Ye have been rebellious against the LORD from the day that I knew you."* (Deuteronomy 9, 22-24)

Enoch: So what exactly happened at Kibrothhattaavah that God was so furious with the Israelites?

TCG: Moses was accusing the Israelites for what God had scolded him for: in Kibrothhattaavah is when the people rebelled against God (and Moses) explicitly.

Enoch: Rebelled? Maybe it was understood as such because they were calling in the names of <u>foreign gods</u>?

TCG: Yes, for all the food that was missing from their diet which they had in Egypt.

Enoch: Were they wrong for doing so? Was God not omnipotent? Did he not provide for their wishes before?

TCG: And he did so again this time as well, they received flocks of quail unto their plates – that's the meat which they were craving for. But the fact remains that they should have been content with what they received and not ask for things which were beyond their grasp.

Enoch: I would respectfully disagree with that statement. Moses and God should have provided for all their needs.

TCG: So you are saying that they should not have a lesson in humility?

Enoch: I do not see what the fuss was all about; God could have provided the Israelites with the Quails, to begin with, why would they be needed to be reeducated?

TCG: This is what the Sanhedrin (the Wisemen Council) was for; it was first formed back then.

Enoch: How did you figure?

TCG: Before Kibrothhattaavah, the Israelites were in a different place and God lost his patience for them. They kept complaining but not to Moses – but God (!)
This is when God's patience ran out completely and he started a fire that burnt them: *"And when the people complained, it displeased the LORD: and the LORD heard it; and his anger was kindled; and the fire of the LORD burnt among them, and consumed them....And the people cried unto Moses; and when Moses prayed unto the LORD, the fire was quenched. And he called the name of the place Taberah: because the fire of the LORD burnt among them."* (Numbers 11, 1-3)

Enoch: But it was hard for them, can they not complain?

TCG: This is what the multitude brought unto the Israelites; naturally, Moses kept blaming the people for what has happened, to deflect the blame from him.

You cannot forget that Moses was denied entry into Canaan due to his transgressions, so he had to keep telling the people it was their fault. So much for an undisputed leader, eh?

Enoch: I still cannot fathom this.

TCG: God now needed to deal with the Israelites, the multitude, the Golden Calf, the burning, the Wisemen Council – this takes us back to Jethro and his council to Moses, does it not?

Enoch: It is hard for me.

TCG: We will continue this in our next message, do not worry your head over this.

The Twenty-First Message - The Secret of the Scriptures

Enoch: You promised me an explanation from the "depths" of this book.

TCG: The more we delve into this last book of the Pentateuch, the more we find new secrets surfacing. Moses has helped us understand how <u>he experiences</u> the Israelites' experience.
We now "expect" and focus on all the clues, "the symbols" and the metaphors along the way. It is not clear to us what has happened and what is but an allegory.

What matters is though is that how The Creator sees and decides what to expose and what to leave in the shadows for a future reveal (if any).

Enoch: I understand what you mean, but it is unclear to me.

TCG: This is "the fog of war" – the battle for perception. Moses has already told us about Kibrothhattaavah, but he has also mentioned "Massah" and "Taberah", among the many sins of the Israelites in a single passage: *"And at Taberah, and at Massah, and at Kibrothhattaavah, ye provoked the Lord to wrath."* (Deuteronomy 9, 22)

Enoch: As usual.

TCG: Let us first explain what happened at each place: at Massah, the Israelites complained about the lack of water; this is where Moses was told to use his staff and hit the rock for water to come out of it. (Exodus 17, 1-6)

Enoch: And what is their crime, for trying God and see if he does exist? Because they complained they had to die?! Shame!

TCG: In Taberah, the Israelites were just complaining, so God had burnt a few acres of that camp, with these people in it. They cried out to Moses and Moses prayed to God and the fire died out.

Enoch: And again I ask, what is their sin to deserve the death penalty? They were enduring the hardships of the road, it was not easy for them. How is this not excess brutality on God's behalf? Why did he even deliver them from Egypt if he wanted to kill them in the wilderness?

And at Kibrothhattaavah? Some of the people were praying for some meat and vegetables. God had killed many of them, as punishment for their ungratefulness, not to mention their complaints.

Enoch: So this was a massacre.

TCG: It appears so, but there is another depth here that you are missing. Let us understand the profound nature of this and you would too understand Enoch: this déjà vu.

Enoch: What are you talking about?

TCG: Here is the first clue: *"Then said the Lord unto Moses, Behold, I will rain bread from heaven for you...And it shall come to pass, that on the sixth day they shall prepare that which they bring in; and it shall be twice as much as they gather daily...And Moses said, This shall be, when the Lord shall give you in the evening flesh to eat, and in the morning bread to the full...And Moses spake unto Aaron, Say unto all the congregation of the children of Israel, Come near before the Lord: for he hath heard your murmurings...speak unto them, saying, At even ye shall eat flesh, and in the morning ye shall be filled with bread; and ye shall know that I am the Lord your God."* (Exodus 16, 4-12)

Enoch: And their punishment?

TCG: No punishment; only a blessing.

Enoch: Fine, then why were they rationed? Why could they not continue picking food after the morning and after the evening?

TCG: They were not rationed; they had that food as long as they needed it. Why then did they decide to complain and murmur to God at Kibrothhattaavah?

This is the déjà vu I was talking about: did it matter what happened there or was there an underlying announcement, much greater than the incident? A dream of sorts of Moses which was planted by God in his mind perhaps...?

Enoch: What are you saying?

TCG: Does it strike you as logical for God to smite the Israelites for asking meat? Does it seem plausible to you that they complain about what they must now endure, God listens, intervenes and smite them? We are misunderstanding the entire situation.

Enoch: Then what the hell is going on here exactly?!

TCG: Kibrothhattaavah is an allegory. What we think was written or what is presently "seen" by Moses and others did not take place. This is how God relays his messages.

Enoch: Fine, please explain what it means then.

TCG: Next time.

The Twenty-Second Message - Why an allegory?

TCG: I can already surmise what it is you wish to ask me: how is it that what we see never took place, right?

Enoch: Yes, pretty much.

TCG: Each person, as well as his/her leaders (or God[s]) has a "weak spot".

These weak spots are there to be pressed and make people do what it is that you wish them to do.

Enoch: Can life not be simpler with everything already determined in a linear fashion?

TCG: Yes, it can be but the beauty is for people to be able to understand which is the **true way** and which is the way, laid in front of them. It is not always clear.

Enoch: "Means to an end"?

TCG: Precisely. So what are Kibrothhattaavah? What is their purpose in understanding the rise of The Nation of Israel?

Enoch: What "nation"? They are people wandering in the desert.

TCG: Foundations and infrastructures of nations were erected long before these nations had already been founded. Even Israel, which was declared as a nation in 1948 had the infrastructure for such a nation at least 40 years prior. It already had a militia, councils, ministries of sorts – how would the people founding that nation be able to create these out of thin air?

Enoch: What are you talking about? What does this have anything to do with what happened at Kibrothhattaavah?

TCG: It does not matter if Kibrothhattaavah had happened, it is not even important. What matters is that God found the pretence to establish the first council, the Sanhedrin of the Israelites which later became the modern parliament of Israel, The Knesset. This was already established in Numbers 11, 11: *"And Moses said unto the Lord, Wherefore hast thou afflicted thy servant? and wherefore have I not found favour in thy sight, that thou layest the burden of all this people upon me?"*

Enoch: So it was Moses now complaining, eh? Hehe.

TCG: This is what God wanted: for Moses to not be able to stand firm, so there would be an infrastructure in place for a Nation instead of Moses.

Enoch: How do you surmise that?

TCG: God has left everything; he did not supply the meat to the people and told Moses to: *"Gather unto me seventy men of the elders of Israel, whom thou knowest to be the elders of the people, and officers over them; and bring them unto the tabernacle of the congregation, that they may stand there with thee."* (Numbers 11, 16) Only after this assignment, did God continue delivering the meat to the Israelites. Do you now understand Enoch? God put this pressure on Moses so he would snap and ask for aid. This is exactly how the Sanhedrin came to be: God saw that Moses was unable to withstand the pressure and was now needed to find "a replacement" for Moses as the leader of the Israelites.

Enoch: I am sorry, I find this a tad hard to believe. Why are we speaking about this in Deuteronomy?

TCG: Moses had selective memory:

1. Moses only remembered what he wanted to remember.
2. It was also for us to see what happened and why.

Enoch: You have intrigued me, when did the seeds had started being planted by God?

TCG: When Jethro came.

One must ask him/herself this question: how did Jethro find Moses in the middle of the wilderness, so far away from his home?

We know for certain that Moses was busy leading the people, had no spare time for lectures and most definitely did not find the time for his wife or his children. Moses did not even recognize Jethro at first, as it was written: *"And he said unto Moses, I thy father in law Jethro am come unto thee, and thy wife, and her two sons with her."* (Exodus 18, 6) Was Jethro "a messenger" and not himself?

<u>Enoch:</u> What do you mean? Why would Jethro bother coming?

<u>TCG:</u> To give advice? To erect the courthouses, no: *"What is this thing that thou doest to the people? why sittest thou thyself alone, and all the people stand by thee from morning unto even...When they have a matter, they come unto me; and I judge between one and another, and I do make them know the statutes of God, and his laws. And Moses' father in law said unto him, The thing that thou doest is not good. Thou wilt surely wear away, both thou, and this people that is with thee: for this thing is too heavy for thee; thou art not able to perform it thyself alone...I will give thee counsel, and God shall be with thee...And thou shalt teach them ordinances and laws, and shalt shew them the way wherein they must walk, and the work that they must do. Moreover thou shalt provide out of all the people able men, such as fear God...and place such over them, to be rulers of thousands...And let them judge the people at all seasons...If thou shalt do this thing, and God command thee so, then thou shalt be able to endure, and all this people shall also go to their place in peace."* (Exodus 18, 14-23)

Did Jethro stay? No, we know that he was sent back by Moses to his land. How is it that Jethro came by himself and did not bring Moses' family with him?

Enoch: You ask humble questions to which I do not know the answer. Please explain.

TCG: Next time I will.

The Twenty-Third Message - Moses is playing dirty

Enoch: The plot thickens.

TCG: Last book of the Pentateuch, what did you expect to happen? The main problem with critics is that they try to personify God instead of recognizing his Godhood. God is not like Man – he does whatever he finds right for Man, not the other way around.

Enoch: Fine, but why must people demand water or food? Is it not logical that there is a need to feed this multitude?

TCG: We would address that as well and understand why Moses was playing dirty and why he blames the people for their misfortune, deflecting all blame from him: *"Likewise when the Lord sent you from Kadeshbarnea, saying, Go up and possess the land which I have given you; then ye rebelled against the commandment of the Lord your God...nor hearkened to his voice. Ye have been rebellious against the Lord from the day that I knew you...I fell down before the Lord forty days and forty nights...because the Lord had said he would destroy you."* (Deuteronomy 9, 23-25)

Enoch: In essence, "you should be thankful for me shielding you from harm."

TCG: Precisely, but not exactly – where was a rebellion? In Kadeshbarnea; the rebel was Moses, who was instructed to hit the rock for the water to come out of it. But, due to his lack of faith in The Lord, was denied entry to The Promised Land.

We must not also forget about the people's attitude post-Spy Saga. The people were in complete hysteria, where could they go? Where can they go? It was enough for God to decide that this generation would not enter The Promised Land.

Enoch: It seems to me that God exploited the circumstances anywhere they went, so he could get rid of the Older Generation, including Moses, Miriam and Aaron. Moses blames the people for his misfortune as if he was not to be blamed for it. As if he did not walk with them all this time – preposterous!

TCG: It is written so <u>we could believe</u> it was so. The people was going through a reeducation period, so they could accept the Laws of God, the much-needed fidelity towards him and the ability to survive in the wilderness, to harden these "spoiled brats". This is exactly why they were denied water and other basic needs.

However, this is but a metaphor for what he expected them to be – frugal with their supplies so they may conquer the land and control it.

Enoch: And Moses was not aware of it?

TCG: Likely, he was not, as he had tremendous pride in his position and responsibility.

Enoch: What about transparency? Towards the people?

TCG: Was Man punished? Let us see:

1. *"And I will establish my covenant with you, neither shall all flesh be cut off any more by the waters of a flood; neither shall there any more be a flood to destroy the earth." (Genesis 9, 11)* This is the First Covenant between God and humanity.

2. *"In the same day the LORD made a covenant with Abram, saying, Unto thy seed have I given this land, from the river of Egypt unto the great river, the river Euphrates:"* (Genesis 15, 18) The Second Covenant between God and humanity, this time choosing a people.

3. *"I am the LORD God of Abraham thy father, and the God of Isaac: the land whereon thou liest, to thee will I give it, and to thy seed; And thy seed shall be as the dust of the earth, and thou shalt spread abroad...and in thee and in thy seed shall all the families of the earth be blessed."* (Genesis 13, 15, Genesis 28, 13-14) A Third Covenant, between Abraham's seed, which includes the Israelites (sons of Jacob), the Edomites (sons of Esau, Jacob's brother), the Ishmaelites (sons of Ishmael, Abraham's son and Isaac's half-brother) – all the Semites together.

Enoch: Are these carved in stone? More like carved in ice.

TCG: These are covenants, God is infallible and <u>does not break his promises</u>: he can punish, harm, smite but the end resolution is that he would always promise – by miracle or by other means.

Enoch: And what is the overall message?

TCG: That everything <u>has already taken place</u>. There was never a people who has never had the danger of extermination at their tracks.

The Twenty-Fourth Message - The Secret

TCG: *"Therefore shall ye keep all the commandments which I command you this day, that ye may be strong, and go in and possess the land...which the LORD sware unto your fathers to give unto them and to their seed, a land that floweth with milk and honey."* (Deuteronomy 11, 8-9) I know that there seems to be a repetition, but there is a reason for the nuances here.

Enoch: I do not see much of a difference, to be honest.

TCG: Moses has let his mouth run, but the people do not seem to tell the difference, which is why no questions were asked in regards to it. Let us focus: at first, the Israelites were blamed for any transgression given, where God commands the people to do anything he asks of them since these commands are "holy".
The man in charge of this "belief in blame" was no other than Moses with his tribal council (The Levites) and his own family, who are essentially the priesthood. Everything was done to ensure that it was blind faith. God led the people to The Promised Land: *"And thou shalt teach them diligently unto thy children, and shalt talk of them when thou sittest in thine house, and when thou walkest by the way, and when thou liest down, and when thou risest up."* (Deuteronomy 6, 7) And why? So the people would be busy following God's commands and not question God's judgement. God would supply the people with everything they need.

Enoch: Put one's trust in The Lord?

TCG: *"The LORD is my shepherd; I shall not want. He maketh me to lie down in green pastures: he leadeth me beside the still waters...Yea, though I walk through the valley of the shadow of death, I will fear no evil: for thou art with me; thy rod and thy staff they comfort me."* (Psalm 23, 1-4)

Enoch: So God is both the rod as well as the comfort. What about free will?

TCG: God makes people think they are in control of what they do. In control of their destiny, but God is the one to decide upon the Path of Man.

Enoch: So Man is but a putty?

TCG: You thought differently?

Enoch: So why must the people endure this and follow all of God's commands then?

TCG: Let us go over God's "manipulation" for the past 40 years of walking the wilderness, shall we?

1. The Israelites were only able to leave Egypt when God wished them to.
2. They left Egypt while the Egyptian army drowned – the might of God.
3. They took a long detour through Philistine land, so they may not miss Egypt.
4. The Amalekites thinned their herd (an enemy to hate).
5. No water, no food. Reeducation in the making.
6. No food, no vegetables. Missing Egypt – keep going towards their goal.
7. The Sin of the Spies, a trap laid by God to see how faithful they are.
8. Punishment: the Old Generation would perish while the younger one enters.

Enoch: But these are facts. What is the point here?

TCG: Egypt was a much better land for the Israelites than Canaan was, that is what <u>Moses said</u>. People do not miss places where it was bad for them, that is a fact. Yes, the Israelites worked hard to leave Egypt <u>but they never asked to leave in the first place.</u>

After the Sin of the Spies, the people wanted to return to Egypt. God could not afford this. Did he decide that Canaan was to be conquered for their sake? No – <u>for his sake</u>, as God needed to make true to his word.

Enoch: I think I understand it now.

TCG: It was easier to kill the Old Generation who still remembered Egypt than to carve Egypt out of their hearts. The Young Generation had no idea what Egypt looked or felt like – they were born in the wilderness.

Enoch: And that is the big secret?

TCG: It appears most people who read The Scriptures have no idea what is written in them, then I would say that is a pretty big secret, yes.

The Twenty-Fifth Message - Blessings (and curses?)

Enoch: It looks like Moses just could not take any accountability for what has happened to the people.

TCG: He meant well, but we need to understand the meaning of the actions taken: *"Therefore shall ye lay up these my words in your heart and in your soul, and bind them for a sign upon your hand...And ye shall teach them your children, speaking of them when thou sittest in thine house...and when thou risest up. And thou shalt write them upon the door posts of thine house...That your days may be multiplied, and the days of your children, in the land which the LORD sware unto your fathers to give them, as the days of heaven upon the earth."* (Deuteronomy 11, 18-21) In essence, Moses both blessed as well as cursed in the name of God.

Enoch: So Moses has made everyone pious.

TCG: Not everyone, only the men are obligated by this. There is total disregard towards the women, and had he meant the entire family – he would have said so.
Moses was doing everything for people to remember the commands of God with symbolism, mostly physical so it would be easier to remember.

Enoch: The day-to-day teachings I understand stem from these.

TCG: Here is now the warnings Moses was giving to the people: *"Behold, I set before you this day a blessing and a curse; A blessing, if ye obey the commandments of the LORD your God...And a curse, if ye will not obey the commandments of the LORD...but turn aside out of the way which I command you this day, to go after other gods, which ye have not known."* (Deuteronomy 11, 26-28)

Enoch: How could he say that?

TCG: There is symbiosis: do as I say and I will repay you handsomely; let yourselves be led astray and worship other gods, and I shall smite you. The carrot and the stick.

Enoch: You are the only ones responsible for your own lives then, eh?

TCG: One may look at that way, yes. Moses now implied that all statutes of the idols should be destroyed. He also marked the spots in which people may now sacrifice and eat the sacrifices; anything else is off-limits: *"But unto the place which the* Lord *your God shall choose out of all your tribes to put his name there, even unto his habitation shall ye seek...And there ye shall eat before the* Lord *your God, and ye shall rejoice in all that ye put your hand unto...wherein the* Lord *thy God hath blessed thee. Ye shall not do after all the things that we do here this day, every man whatsoever is right in his own eyes."* (Deuteronomy 12, 5, 7-8)

Enoch: So there are certain places where people may eat, yes? God chooses the place for the tribe to dwell and they are not allowed to eat from the sacrifice except there, correct?

TCG: Yes. Remember also that these commands are aimed at the men and boys, but the entire family is commanded to sit there and eat. No exceptions.

Enoch: So, God chooses the place and time of the sacrifice, people are obligated to sit there and eat from the sacrifice, which brings them closer to God as they "break bread" together. And naturally, they cannot worship and false idols in God's eyes.

TCG: Correct.

Enoch: Dictatorship.

TCG: Theocracy.

Enoch: Semantics; Moses elevated himself above the people, since the priesthood belongs to his own family, his tribe.

TCG: God is what matters here; the loyalty of Man is to God; it supersedes any loyalty one might have to one's family. People must obey God and the faith: *"If thy brother...or thy son, or thy daughter, or the wife...or thy friend, which is as thine own soul, entice thee secretly...Let us go and serve other gods, which thou hast not known...Namely, of the gods of the people which are round about you...Thou shalt not consent unto him, nor hearken unto him...But thou shalt surely kill him; thine hand shall be first upon him to put him to death, and afterwards the hand of all the people. And thou shalt stone him with stones, that he die; because he hath sought to thrust thee away from the LORD thy God, which brought thee out of the land of Egypt, from the house of bondage."* (Deuteronomy 13, 6-10)

Enoch: Gruesome. People should kill their own family; blind obedience to God. This is what happened when dark regimes rose up, no? Children informed the authorities of their parents' murmurs of revolution. It is even considered fine to slaughter people: *"If thou shalt hear say in one of thy cities, which the LORD thy God hath given thee to dwell there, saying, Certain men, the children of Belial, are gone out from among you, and have withdrawn the inhabitants of their city, saying, Let us go and serve other gods...Then shalt thou enquire, and make search, and ask diligently...if it be truth, and the thing certain...Thou shalt surely smite the inhabitants of that city with the edge of the sword, destroying it utterly, and all that is therein, and the cattle thereof, with the edge of the sword. And thou shalt gather all the spoil of it into the midst of the street thereof, and shalt burn with fire the city."* (Deuteronomy 13, 12-16)

TCG: People must have something to fear of to conform with what God intends for them.

The Twenty-Sixth Message - Moses and his Reforms

Enoch: So Moses told the people that these are God's words; makes your blood curdle.

TCG: Let me explain to you where this comes from. Moses states that the Israelites are God's children, holy and chosen by God over any other nation, as it appears in Deuteronomy 14, 2.

Enoch: And according to new dietary laws, even vegetables must now be eaten in specific locations chosen by God. Does that make sense to you?

TCG: You are again missing the point: God wishes it. Man does not have any say in the matter. Man does what God says, not the other way around.

Enoch: All of this just so Moses may carry God's favour?

TCG: Moses truly believed that love and dependence on God are unconditional. Moses cannot have found it in his heart to break away:

At first, he did not even want the job – now he cannot fathom anyone replacing him doing so. He believed that he was doing God's work, that's it. If you remember correctly, all sacrifices and eating are to be done in a certain place, while the tithes are to be given at the gates to the widows and the orphans, as well as the Levite who is without land to work and no revenue channels.

Taxation.

However, there is a nuance here as this is not what God had said.

Enoch: What is the difference?

TCG: *"But the seventh year thou shalt let it rest and lie still; that the poor of thy people may eat: and what they leave the beasts of the field shall eat. In like manner thou shalt deal with thy vineyard, and with thy oliveyard."* (Exodus 23, 11) God meant that the leave is to be left there for the taking.

Moses wanted the people to gather the leave and put it at the gates for the widows and orphans to eat.

Enoch: I do not see the odd notion about it.

TCG: It is not odd, it is admirable. It was also a tiny portion in his entire reform in regards to the seventh year: *"And this is the manner of the release: Every creditor that lendeth ought unto his neighbour shall release it; he shall not exact it of his neighbour, or of his brother; because it is called the Lord's release. Of a foreigner thou mayest exact it again: but that which is thine with thy brother thine hand shall release".* (Deuteronomy 15, 2-3)

Enoch: If only the banks had been so kind...but what about the foreigner? Why is the foreigner not released? A tad of bigotry and xenophobia, no?

TCG: God meant that the land should be left to rest, not that people should leave debts to rest.

Enoch: Not a bad reform. He has been living with the Israelites in the wilderness for 40 years. Now he was going soft.

TCG: Not exactly. Moses thought that if he carried favour with the people, he would be able to recarry favour with God and God would allow him in.

Enoch: So this was done not because he thought that it was the right thing to do, but that it was the right thing for him.

TCG: In the first years, Moses was not much of a leader. He did what God told him to do, did not change a thing. Now because he understood that he may not enter Canaan, he tried to change God's decree and to carry favour with the people.

Enoch: And this is from the Jubilee Year mentioned in Leviticus, yes? This is how he made up this new reform?

TCG: *"And ye shall hallow the fiftieth year, and proclaim liberty throughout all the land unto all the inhabitants thereof: it shall be a jubile unto you; and ye shall return every man unto his possession, and ye shall return every man unto his family."* (Leviticus 25, 10) The Servants of God would be free, to some degree.

The Twenty-Seventh Message - Critique about Moses

Enoch: I find it hard to believe that Moses made up all of these commands. Is it not possible that God was feeding him these and he just relayed these to the people?

TCG: I understand where this is coming from. You think that the commands are so intricate and have such a high level of jurisprudence involved that it was unlikely that Moses made these up.

Enoch: To be honest, he does not seem capable of doing so.

TCG: You seem to forget that Moses was an Egyptian prince. The sons of the reigning monarch needed to know everything there was to know about running a nation: economics, the law, military science, agriculture – everything. Does it strike you as odd that Moses was well-versed in these?

Enoch: Yes, it does strike me as odd. He kept silent for 40 years, what made him start speaking so much and explaining God's laws to the people?

TCG: The Israelites were a moment away from entering Canaan; Moses was unable to pass into the land, due to God's decree. He was trying to reverse it as he was chosen by God to lead this nation. He was now trying to make the people think that they are responsible for that fact.

Enoch: But God is infallible. If there is a decree, it cannot be reversed. Moses is not God's lieutenant, he is a prophet, a messenger. Moses cannot change what God had ordered.

TCG: True, so this is why he tried to make the people feel guilty enough to cry out to God and ask Moses to be spared, or so he believed. Then he started speaking about holidays, such as Passover, Sukkot and Pentecost. He made sure people understood that they should rejoice in these holidays, even with the foreigners and slaves among them.

Is it possible that Moses was no longer present when he commanded the people to celebrate?

Enoch: What do you mean? These holidays are still being celebrated every year.

TCG: There are other holidays mentioned in the Pentateuch which are celebrated every year and never mentioned in Deuteronomy; these were mentioned in Leviticus and Numbers and not in Deuteronomy – why so?

Enoch: Dementia? Old age? Moses was already 120 years old.

TCG: Perhaps, but Moses was the one giving a summary of everything else mentioned in the other books of the Pentateuch. It seems unlikely for him to forget **that**.

Enoch: That is a valid point.

The Twenty-Eighth Message - The Teachings of the King

TCG: As you can see, Moses' nationalistic sentiments and zero-tolerance towards idolatry.

Enoch: But that is not up to Moses to decide, God is the one to pass judgment here: *"For I the LORD thy God am a jealous God, visiting the iniquity of the fathers upon the children unto the third and fourth generation of them that hate me."* (Exodus 20, 5) What is Moses trying to do, have people kill in the name of The Lord?

TCG: Precisely: *"Then shalt thou bring forth that man or that woman, which have committed that wicked thing, unto thy gates, even that man or that woman, and shalt stone them with stones, till they die."* (Deuteronomy 17, 5) And I know how cruel this seems, but having family members turn on each other is even worse.

We can also witness that Moses added a religious element should a judge may not pass judgement: *"And the man that will do...and will not hearken unto the priest that standeth to minister there before the LORD...or unto the judge, even that man shall die: and thou shalt put away the evil from Israel...When thou art come unto the land which the LORD thy God giveth thee, and shalt possess it, and shalt dwell therein, and shalt say, I will set a king over me, like as all the nations that are about me;Thou shalt in any wise set him king over thee, whom the LORD thy God shall choose..."* (Deuteronomy 17, 12-15)

Enoch: A king? What king?!

TCG: Moses was quite the prophet, was he not? That is the Judgement of the King. Each nation around the Israelites had a king leading them; the Hebrews though had the Priesthood to govern them. Is it not possible that the Hebrews might want to put a king instead of a priest to govern them, like everyone else? That is exactly why Moses created this "prenuptial agreement" – to avoid any mistakes the people might have in the future. That means that any king chosen, would be superseded by the priesthood – the priests (representing God's Will) would be the ones choosing the right king for the people. Not only that, but the king must be a Hebrew and cannot be of any other ethnicity but Hebrew.

Enoch: I find this redundant; what other nation is there here besides the Hebrews?

TCG: And what is the "mixed multitude"? In regards to kingship, the future "corroborates" the words of Moses: Saul was God's first anointed king, meaning that king's rule with God's approval and his (and his alone's) decision to make them kings over Israel.

Enoch: But how was this possible, even the priesthood was not in place yet.

TCG: Moses saw the kings of the people around the Hebrews, and understood that the Hebrews would like to be the same as any other people. He understood the problems the people would have because Saul was declared King of Israel three times before he was made king. There were many opposing forces to Saul becoming king. This revolutionary approach to leadership in a theocratic society was novel. The first coronation was done in private, where Samuel the prophet, Saul and God were present only. The second one had no opposing parties, nor any claimants to the throne, but Saul was granted the coronation by winning a game of fates, not by virture.

Enoch: Why was Moses dealing with this though?

TCG: Moses had the clairvoyance to the future; he already understood what might happen in the future, hence he wanted to create rules for it:

1. A king by God's Divine Decision, that is, a king appointed by the priesthood.
2. A Hebrew king. By the way, Saul was coronated three times – do you now understand why this was so complex?

Enoch: Fine, but why bother himself with this now?

TCG: It was never dealt with before because it was irrelevant for that time. But, the Hebrews are but a moment away from entering Canaan and conquering the land, so this has become relevant again. He also mentioned that a king should not focus on producing wealth and be humble.

Enoch: That is not a bad thing.

TCG: No, it is not.

The Twenty-Ninth Message - Moses' Teachings

TCG: As you can see, Moses kept creating his own rules and how should one spot False Kings (False Messiahs).

Enoch: A very micro-perspective here contributed by Moses; I am not sure it was relevant for the people at that time.

TCG: But here is a novelty item: Cities of Refuge. Say a person murders another, and the penalty for doing so is death. That man now runs to a City of Refuge before his execution and is then saved. Is this not humane in your eyes?

Enoch: I think that a murderer should die.

TCG: I am not referring to premeditated murder. I am speaking about a person who accidentally killed another.

Enoch: You mean manslaughter, as opposed to a murder?

TCG: *"And this is the case of the slayer, which shall flee thither, that he may live: Whoso killeth his neighbour ignorantly, whom he hated not in time past."* (Deuteronomy 19, 4) This refers to people who killed people without prior intention of doing so, the person who has murdered them would be spared ("Eye for an Eye Principle" would not be in effect), but Moses leaves the concept of blood feud in effect: *"But if any man hate his neighbour...and smite him mortally that he die, and fleeth into one of these cities: Then the elders of his city shall send and fetch him thence, and deliver him into the hand of the avenger of blood, that he may die."* (Deuteronomy 19, 11-12)

Enoch: So blood feuds are still on the table.

TCG: The Scriptures are very cautious here: *"If a false witness rise up against any man to testify against him that which is wrong; Then both the men, between* *whom the controversy is, shall stand before the* LORD, *before the priests and the judges, which shall be in those days."* (Deuteronomy 19, 17) A person could not be condemned to death based on the testimony of a single witness. There must be at least two.

Enoch: Moses also mentioned other rules, in regards to the priests' roles in warfare.

TCG: Yes, but these are not as interesting as other rules of war. We already know that when the priests call for war, God wishes it and people must go to war.

However, there are always certain clauses which allow people to be "draft dodgers". A person who has recently built a house, may stay in his house.

Also, it is always better to call for peace than for war, in the army can: *"When thou comest nigh unto a city to fight against it, then proclaim peace unto it."* (Deuteronomy 20, 10)

Enoch: A tad poetic, if I may say so.

TCG: This is a biblical style of peace, not what you think. This peace brings humiliation galore (and bondage): *"And it shall be, if it make thee answer of peace, and open unto thee, then it shall be, that all the people that is found therein shall be tributaries unto thee, and they shall serve thee."* (Deuteronomy 20, 11)

Enoch: Sounds more of a Fight or Flight kind of raw deal, not much of a "peace offering".

TCG: Agreed, but this is Moses' notion of peace between the people. Remember what was laid in front of them: *"When the* LORD *thy God hath cut off the nations, whose land the* LORD *thy God giveth thee, and thou succeedest them, and* *dwellest in their cities, and in their houses; But the women, and the little ones, and the cattle, and all that is in the city, even all the spoil thereof, shalt thou take unto thyself; and thou shalt eat the spoil of thine enemies, which the Lord thy God hath given thee."* (Deuteronomy 19, 1; 20, 14)

<u>Enoch:</u> "Spoils of war"?

<u>TCG:</u> Yes, women were property and spoils of war, same as cattle or jewellery. You cannot judge the old days with a modern perspective of things.

The Thirtieth Message - The Rules of War

TCG: It is imperative to take notice of the nuances here, you would learn a lot.

Enoch: I would appreciate an explanation of this immensely.

TCG: It is not the easiest to explain, but Moses presents most of these rules as if they were given to him by the heavens, but that is not true.

Enoch: What are you saying?

TCG: Moses is drafting his own strategy, presenting it as advice to the newly appointed warlord, Joshua, who was chosen by God to lead the Israelites.

Enoch: I have noticed that but what was Moses' intention?

TCG: Once Moses decided to circumvent Joshua, speaking to the people directly before the battle, it was implied to them that Moses was the one advising Joshua, which made him relevant in the eyes of the people and created an internal dissonance. This is no more than a ruse created by Moses, which is no more than a power trip perpetrated by Moses to continue ruling the Israelites.

Enoch: So Joshua was coerced to take Moses' advice.

TCG: The answer to this question is in the Book of Exodus: *"But against any of the children of Israel shall not a dog move his tongue, against man or beast."* (Exodus 11, 7) That means there was "bribery" involved here.

Enoch: What bribery is that?

TCG: Joshua had fewer soldiers to use, as all the old, lame and the ones who built themselves a house or whatnot were now taken away from him. Moses was now offering these soldiers incentives in the form of spoils of war, including the women of their enemies.

Enoch: What else could he have promised them then?

TCG: Nationalism, loyalty and worshipping God? Just to name a few here, where the spoils of war go directly to the Tabernacle, that is to God as a tribute and nothing else? This lesson Moses learnt from the gentiles, this is not the Israelite way.

Enoch: What are you saying then?

TCG: That all that Moses is trying to command people to do, would not happen. Furthermore, it only angers God. Moses pays this no heed since he knows that he would die in the wilderness anyway, so why not try this option?

Enoch: Quite the tall tale; how do you know this?

TCG: Do you remember asking me who exactly wrote Deuteronomy? Were these the words of God or Moses'? Did Moses dictate his words to someone else on his deathbed?

Enoch: And do you know the answer to this question? Can you prove this?

TCG: I certainly can, but I would need to move in time to show you who wrote the book, but that is a story for another time. Just remember what the soldiers were offered to fight.

Enoch: Soldiers of fortune; it was common until the modern era.

TCG: Yes, but there is a sentiment behind Moses' words and a point to this story.

Everything Moses planned and commanded, these rules were made for distant cities; on the outskirts of The Promised Land within Canaan.

Enoch: Is that a bad thing?

TCG: God and the people had good interests; the gentiles? Less so: *"But thou shalt utterly destroy them...as the* Lord *thy God hath commanded thee:That they teach you not to do after all their abominations, which they have done unto their* *gods; so should ye sin against the* Lord *your God."* (Deuteronomy 20, 18) God is at the top of the hierarchy.

Enoch: Before the money.

TCG: Yes, but Moses finishes his sermon in a practical and environmental step, which shows us his great wisdom: *"When thou shalt besiege a city a long time, in making war against it to take it, thou shalt not destroy the trees thereof by forcing an axe against them: for thou mayest eat of them."* (Deuteronomy 20, 19)

Enoch: Poetic.

The Thirty-First Message - The Building of a Nation

TCG: Before we start criticizing Moses, we need to first understand his motives: Moses thought of himself as a "prophet" or "the architect of the settlement" of this great nation, if you will. Up until this point, all commandments given were private, in between this person or the next – nothing which obliged the entire nation.

Yes, indeed, Moses did not receive these commandments from God, but a nation in the making needs rules, laws and regulations to follow.

Enoch: So you are saying that Moses did not receive these commandments straight from the word of God – how could you possibly know that? It is even written that he was standing in front of The Lord.

TCG: I am referring to the commandments laid in front of us in Deuteronomy, not laws passed and presented to us in previous books.

Enoch: So please explain yourself. We need to understand what was said and what Moses meant.

TCG: Moses, as you can see, was summarising everything that has happened to the Israelites in the wilderness. He was chronicling all that has happened to them for future generations as well, so they may never forget where they came from.

By doing so, he noticed that the Israelites were missing guidelines with which they may build that nation. Every nation needs a set of rules to follow. God was providing for them up until now; but, the time has come for them to govern themselves without God's chaperoning them.

Enoch: And again I ask, how could you possibly know the words spoken unto the ears of Moses were not the words of God? How do you know it was all a figment of his imagination?

TCG: I will accept your challenge. Let us move forward, the capture of Jericho. Moses is long gone. So, in the Book of Joshua, we find that the strategic plan to capture the city was laid out in front of us. So what exactly could we find there to corroborate what I am saying: *"And the LORD said unto Joshua, See, I have given into thine hand Jericho, and the king thereof, and the mighty men of valour."* (Joshua 6, 2) We notice that Joshua was not following Moses' teachings, as Joshua (nor his emissaries) pleaded with the city officials to surrender to them. It means that God was not the one to teach Moses the Rules of War. Let us keep reading, shall we: *"And they utterly destroyed all that was in the city, both man and woman, young and old, and ox, and sheep...And they burnt the city with fire, and all that was therein: only the silver, and the gold, and the vessels of brass and of iron, they put into the treasury of the house of the LORD."* (Joshua 6, 21-24) Everyone was slain, including the livestock and every piece of property was confiscated. Moses declared that all loot would be divided between the soldiers, no? Was anything divided between anyone? Seems not. It means that the city was sacked, but not for payment for fighting, but The Tabernacle.

Enoch: You are right, Moses said himself that the loot would be given to the soldiers.

TCG: God thought different; Joshua and the people follow God's commands, not Moses'. It appears that a lot of what Moses had taught them was no more than his own agenda. However, we need to know what happened to the ones that indeed followed Moses' words: *"But the children of Israel committed a trespass in the accursed thing: for Achan, the son of Carmi, the son of Zabdi, the son of Zerah, of the tribe of Judah, took of the accursed thing: and the anger of the LORD was kindled against the children of Israel."* (Joshua 7, 1)

Enoch: I do not understand; he was following Moses' teachings.

TCG: And so God punished them all and they were not able to capture Ai.

Enoch: But why?

TCG: *"Israel hath sinned, and they have also transgressed my covenant which I commanded them: for they have even taken of the accursed thing, and have also stolen, and dissembled also, and they have put it even among their own stuff."* (Joshua 7, 11) It was forbidden loot which they had taken unto themselves, against the covenant between God and the Israelites.

Enoch: So why would Moses say otherwise?

TCG: Do you know what has happened to the looter?

Enoch: Executed?

TCG: God wanted to set rules in which one cannot loot for oneself solely, but for God and thus Achan was: *"And all Israel stoned him with stones, and burned them with fire, after they had stoned them with stones."* (Joshua 7, 25) He was executed alright, alongside his wife, his children and his house. Everyone was paying the piper. Do you now understand what God thought of Moses' laws, Enoch?

Enoch: I find it hard to believe that God would allow Moses to say what he wanted to say then.

TCG: Maybe so, but Moses was a deadman anyway – why not let him say his last words?

The Thirty-Second Message - Waging war and conquest

Enoch: I have noticed that Moses offered alternatives to war. It looks like he divided those wars into Justified Wars and Wars.

TCG: What do you mean?

Enoch: It clearly states in Deuteronomy that: *"When thou comest nigh unto a city to fight against it, then proclaim peace unto it."* (Deuteronomy 20, 10) This is a War since these cities were not in the reach of The Promised Land; that is at least how I understand it.

TCG: And the wars to conquer Canaan, how would they be waged according to Moses?

Enoch: *"But of the cities of these people, which the Lord thy God doth give thee for an inheritance, thou shalt save alive nothing that breatheth."* (Deuteronomy 20, 16)

TCG: *"That they teach you not to do after all their abominations, which they have done unto their gods; so should ye sin against the Lord your God."* (Deuteronomy 20, 18) That is how the passage ends. I know what you are thinking, thence stems this: *"And the city shall be accursed, even it, and all that are therein, to the Lord."* (Joshua 6, 17) Is that what Moses said? No. They then proceeded to slay the entire city, including the livestock. Could they not have spared those animals? Repurpose them to their own needs? Does it make sense to you? Would the Israelites now dwell in these accursed cities?

Enoch: *"...only the silver, and the gold, and the vessels of brass and of iron, they put into the treasury of the house of the Lord."* (Joshua 6, 24) The precious metals were used for religious purposes. But, it is plausible idols were forged in gold in between them, no?

TCG: True, but only the best was given unto God for The Tabernacle, that is for building it the right way. But we digress. There are also other Rules of

War depicted here: *"When thou goest forth to war...And seest among the captives a beautiful woman, and hast a desire unto her, that thou wouldest have her to thy wife"*. (Deuteronomy 21, 10-11)

Enoch: A female prisoner of war.

TCG: And what does Moses think of this? What is the "opportunity" which he saw here? Moses is even magnanimous here.

Enoch: More like a wretch.

TCG: Agreed, this is not familiar to the way of the Israelites, and she would probably teach her progeny about the idols on which she grew up, not God. And Moses continued speaking about the fact that she may have a whole month to mourn her parents.

Enoch: And when the month is up?

TCG: *"...and after that thou shalt go in unto her, and be her husband, and she shall be thy wife."* (Deuteronomy 21, 13) Moses thought of his laws as benevolent, which resembles the Moses we have grown to adore – could it be? And here is another law out of the figment of his imagination: *"If a man have a stubborn and rebellious son, which will not obey the voice of his father, or the voice of his mother...Then shall his father and his mother lay hold on him, and bring him out unto the elders of his city, ...And all the men of his city shall stone him with stones, that he die: so shalt thou put evil away from among you; and all Israel shall hear, and fear."* (Deuteronomy 21, 18-21)

Enoch: Cast the evil out? So brutally?

TCG: This rule of fear is how leaders were able to control their people for years.

Enoch: And the leader of the Chosen People spoke this way? This is not the Moses I know.

TCG: This is not a leader speaking; these rules were created by gentiles surrounding the Israelites.

Enoch: And what could the people do? Moses "lost it".

TCG: And now, do you understand, why The Lord let Moses speak this way and did not execute him immediately? God wanted Moses to harm his own reputation in the eyes of his people, who were in fear of the dire consequences of his laws. We will soon understand that God had never made these laws. But remember, a similar notion would rise later with Elijah, who also did not understand what God had intended hence he also "had to go".

The Thirty-Third Message - The women are not spared either

Enoch: I see you are not explaining everything and skipping chapters here and there. I have noticed that in the past as well, how so?

TCG: I do not find it relevant to waste time explaining things which are clearly "do" and "do not" commandments. As long as people obey these, why would anyone care?

Enoch: But is it not about obeying the rules given to us?

TCG: All this time, and still you do not seem to grasp that Man may try to follow God's commandments, but if Man would not understand them – Man cannot follow them. I will give you a simple example which anyone could understand without further clarification: *"The woman shall not wear that which pertaineth unto a man, neither shall a man put on a woman's garment: for all that do so are abomination unto the LORD thy God."* (Deuteronomy 22, 5) Do you need further clarification on what is written here? A man should dress as a man, a woman should dress as a woman – simple as that.

Enoch: I suppose not.

TCG: But here is a commandment which requires clarification: *"Thou shalt not plow with an ox and an ass together. Thou shalt not wear a garment of divers sorts, as of woollen and linen together."* (Deuteronomy 22, 10-11) The point here is that the ass, which is a weaker animal, should not work alongside the ox, the stronger of the two. Because it is inhumane to make it work the same way. As for the threads, there are two reasons for this:

1. *"Ye shall keep my statutes. Thou shalt not let thy cattle gender with a diverse kind: thou shalt not sow thy field with mingled seed: neither shall a garment mingled of linen and woollen come upon thee."* (Leviticus 19, 19) That is, the Divine Law in practice and keep pure anywhere you go.

2. Because the priests' garments were made of different threads, to distinguish between them – only they were allowed to were different threaded clothes.

Enoch: I see now, that makes sense.

TCG: But not all laws were easy to comprehend (on the mind or the heart). Let us assume a man married a woman and he was discontent with her, what could he do? Let us assume he married a woman whom he thought was a virgin and turns out she was not so and had already fornicated with other men before marrying him. Now, he wishes to divorce her, that is to ask the people to put enough pressure as to allow him to divorce or have the marriage annulled. But, what could the woman's parents do to keep her interests intact, no to mention their reputation?

Enoch: So what is Moses' suggestion?

TCG: Inconceivable; after the young couple retires to their consummation room, the parents would then take the bride's dress for safekeeping with the virgin blood on it, as proof: *"Then shall the father of the damsel, and her mother, take and bring forth the tokens of the damsel's virginity unto the elders of the city in the gate".* (Deuteronomy 22, 15)

Enoch: And is this not degrading? Does her word that she is a virgin not proof enough of her being one?

TCG: And what if the boy lied? *"...And, lo, he hath given occasions of speech against her, saying, I found not thy daughter a maid; and yet these are the tokens of my daughter's virginity. And they shall spread the cloth before the elders of the city. And the elders of that city shall take that man and chastise him; And they shall amerce him in an hundred shekels of silver, and give them unto the father of the* *damsel, because he hath brought up an evil name upon a virgin of Israel: and she shall be his wife; he may not put her away all his days."* (Deuteronomy 22, 16-19)

Enoch: What kind of a law is this? He does not understand anything about relationships and his laws are draconian.

TCG: Exactly; it is not just the man who must now pay a fine for spreading lies about his wife, but also the fact that she must now live with him for the rest of her life. A trustless marriage with a man she hates.

Enoch: And what if the boy was speaking the truth?

TCG: *"But if this thing be true... Then they shall bring out the damsel to the door of her father's house, and the men of her city shall stone her with stones that she die: because she hath wrought folly in Israel, to play the whore in her father's house: so shalt thou put evil away from among you."* (Deuteronomy 22, 20-21)

Enoch: Night and day in comparison with what would happen to the boy if he lies. And these are laws which you say are Moses', not God's.

TCG: Moses tried to interpret the laws of God with his own understanding of the law. This though is not unlike what Moses wishes – for the Israelites to be completely pure and cast out all evil among them. Moreover, should a couple be engaged and the man would fornicate with the engaged woman, they both be put to death. But, what would happen to a man who rapes a virgin who is not engaged? What do you think his sentence would be?

Enoch: A fine?

TCG: True, but only a partial one: *"If a man find a damsel that is a virgin, which is not ... Then the man that lay with her shall give unto the damsel's father fifty* *shekels of silver, and she shall be his wife; because he hath humbled her, he may not put her away all his days."* (Deuteronomy 22, 28-29)

Enoch: *"Hast thou killed, and also taken possession?"* (1 Kings 21, 19)

TCG: Moses intended that all eligible men should marry virgins solely, even if that virgin was no longer one since she was raped.

Enoch: But giving her to her rapist?! Did she not have rights?

TCG: Not in those times; women were property. You cannot forget what happened when Amnon fell in love with Tamar, his half-sister. Amnon raped her after seducing her under false pretences, and when the deed was done – he cast her away. She begged him to marry her, as was customary back then: *"And when she had brought them unto him to eat, he took hold of her, and said unto her...And she answered him...Now therefore, I pray thee, speak unto the king; for he will not withhold me from thee...Then Amnon hated her exceedingly; so that the hatred wherewith he hated her was greater than the love wherewith he had loved her. And Amnon said unto her, Arise, be gone."* (2 Samuel 13, 11-15) As you can see, it is the same way Moses commanded the Israelites.

Enoch: I see now, yes.

The Thirty-Fourth Message - The Vile Swine

TCG: Enoch, you have previously mentioned that I do not usually stumble upon each and every verse, but only certain parts which I find of relevant "added value", that is the ones which I think people might benefit from knowing. In most cases, there are terms which we were taught wrongly about and as such, created different motives in the lives of billions of people in the past two millennia: *"And the swine, though he divide the hoof, and be clovenfooted, yet he cheweth not the cud; he is unclean to you."* (Leviticus 11, 7) but, other animals which were as unclean are not considered as vile as the swine, such as the hare, the camel or the coney.

Enoch: So what is it with the comparison?

TCG: The swine is no viler than the hare, so why is it interpreted that he is?

Enoch: I have no idea.

TCG: It does not appear that the swine is considered vile because it does not ruminate; other animals do not ruminate, none of them is interpreted as vile as the swine. It appears there is a certain prohibition about eating the swine which is not in effect on the others.

Enoch: I always thought that the swine was forbidden because it was vile, not because of his actual traits (or lack of them).

TCG: The reason for it is that it is considered unclean since it is an omnivore, that is an animal which eats everything and is thus considered "vile".

Enoch: That I understand, but how is it that only the swine receives this "special treatment"?

TCG: As you notice, even the author of Leviticus states that the swine parts the hoof, which usually is a trait of a clean animal. But, let us take a further look at The Scriptures to understand this better: *"As a jewel of gold in a swine's snout, so is a fair woman which is without discretion."* (Proverbs 11, 22)

As you can see, the swine is vile and unclean; it creates blemishes where there is perfection. The swine is not just a symbol, but an image: even non-religious individuals may abstain from eating pork, including many denominations of Christianity since the swine is forbidden in both Judaism as well as Islam.

Enoch: It is a known image: "eating like a pig" or "pigging out", as if the swine is a glutton.

TCG: Pretty much; let us move on to another commandment given to the Israelites: *"At the end of three years thou shalt bring forth all the tithe of thine increase the same year, and shalt lay it up within thy gates".* (Deuteronomy 14, 28)

Enoch: Did Moses not forbid people to worship and eat at the gates?

TCG: Very perceptive. What kind of farmer in his right mind would bring forth all of his produce to the gates, for the Levite and the beggar to eat from it? But this has also been mentioned in Leviticus: *"And thou shalt not glean thy vineyard, neither shalt thou gather every grape of thy vineyard; thou shalt leave them for the poor and stranger: I am the LORD your God."* (Leviticus 19, 10) Moses goes against his own teachings, to ease the lives of the less fortunate. I find this benevolent.

The Thirty-Fifth Message - The poor, the bread and the sacrifice

TCG: I know that it may appear as if I am scolding Moses for what he was doing, but my point of being here is to educate. Even Moses understood that birthright and being the firstborn meant a lot to God, which is why he mentioned to them that: *"All the firstling males that come of thy herd and of thy flock thou shalt sanctify unto the LORD thy God: thou shalt do no work with the firstling of thy bullock, nor shear the firstling of thy sheep."* (Deuteronomy 15, 19)

Enoch: I still do not understand the point in this; is an animal, not an animal to be sacrificed anyhow? Why would this matter?

TCG: It matters to God. The fact that the Israelites are God's chosen people, his "firstborn" makes it compelling for them to only sacrifice the firstborn of their flocks based on the massacre of the firstborns of Egypt mentioned in Exodus. This is all symbolic and metaphoric to the connection of the Israelites to God.

Enoch: I understand what he meant now, especially when he spoke about the sacrificial blood which has been a motif for millennia.

TCG: Moses also interpreted why the Israelites were needed to eat Matzot every Passover, to commemorate the fact that they were not able to leaven their bread and enjoy it as they had to leave Egypt in a hurry. It is all symbolic, as you can read here as well: *"Better is a dry morsel, and quietness therewith, than an house full of sacrifices with strife."* (Proverbs 17, 1)

Enoch: Both the morsel, as well as the sacrifice, are mentioned here, poetic – the metaphor has been perfectly hidden within the verse – I am impressed.

But why was Moses so adamant about these laws and rules? Why not focus on laws and rules which would allow the Israelites to rule nations and not just focus on sacrifices and worshipping?

TCG: It may appear as if Moses preferred the Rule of God over the Rule of the King. Do you remember Moses making mention of this to the Israelites?

Enoch: How did you establish that fact?

TCG: It appears to be true; Moses was preaching to the Israelites what a rule should look like. Who did he expect to understand that? So he established the rules of the future: *"Judges and officers shalt thou make thee in all thy gates, which the Lord thy God giveth thee, throughout thy tribes: and they shall judge the people with just judgment. Thou shalt not wrest judgment; thou shalt not respect persons, neither take a gift: for a gift doth blind the eyes of the wise, and pervert the words of the righteous. That which is altogether just shalt thou follow, that thou mayest live, and inherit the land which the Lord thy God giveth thee."* (Deuteronomy 16, 18-20)

The Thirty-Sixth Message - A King in Israel

TCG: The Israelites were required to stand guard, defending God. Whoever dealt with idolatry, even as a crypto-convert, would have been stoned to death. We understand how much Moses was invested in keeping these people as The People of God, he was a true zealot.

Enoch: We can also read about the rules of a monarchy.

TCG: Yes, and how the kings were subordinate to the rules of God and God's work. But, Moses has also given the prerequisite for someone to become a king in Israel:

a. He cannot be a gentile; only an Israelite.

b. He cannot be of great wealth, including a harem.

c. He must be chosen by God or approved by God, not to mention act in God's interests.

Enoch: I can also witness that Moses was against a monarchy, and he found it very "Canaanite".

TCG: *"When thou art come unto the land which the* LORD *thy God giveth thee, and shalt possess it, and shalt dwell therein, and shalt say, I will set a king over me, like as all the nations that are about me."* (Deuteronomy 17, 14)

Enoch: But why was he so adamant about this? The Israelites have not even entered Canaan yet.

TCG: Moses had already understood that eventually, the Israelites would prefer a king over a priest to govern them. Moses believed that the only way in which the Israelites would survive is by the Rule of God through God's priests. God would pave the way for the Israelite's success. Moses was replaced by Joshua, who was not a priest but a general – and this is what a conquering nation needs now – a soldier, not a priest.

Enoch: And were the Rules of the King "invented" by Moses as well? These were not God's instructions? It appears to me that Moses has kept God's interests all along and made the kings subordinate to God's.

TCG: Yes, because many years have passed until the Israelites made a person king of Israel and have tried and each and every other option to govern the people. But, the person who anointed the first king of Israel, duly conferred with Moses' teachings and commandments before doing so: *"Then all the elders of Israel gathered themselves together, and came to Samuel unto Ramah, And said unto him, Behold, thou art old, and thy sons walk not in thy ways: now make us a king to judge us like all the nations. But the thing displeased Samuel, when they said, Give us a king to judge us. And Samuel prayed unto the LORD."* (1 Samuel 8, 4-6)

Enoch: True, but you have mentioned that the people were disappointed with the priests who have become powerful and corrupted, so why would they not go on that path? The people who made the actual appeal to Samuel <u>were the elders, not the people.</u>

TCG: And what do you think of that? Despite the not so bright future, did Samuel give in to their demand?

Enoch: We know there were kings.

TCG: But Samuel did not wish for his people to be like all people. On the other hand, he did not want to make that choice alone and had to confer with a higher power: *"And the LORD said unto Samuel, Hearken unto the voice of the people in all that they say unto thee: for they have not rejected thee, but they have rejected me, that I should not reign over them."* (1 Samuel 8, 7) God realised that the only way in which his commandments would go about is if the people would receive a king anointed by a prophet, which means that the king has been approved by God.

Enoch: So that was how it came to be?

TCG: Yes. Moses had already understood that one day, the priesthood would fail so he needed to make up rules for the monarchy to obey and be second only to God. He knew that otherwise, the people would be divided, civil unrest and war might break out and most importantly – the Israelites would then be found weaker in the eyes of their enemies.

Enoch: So Samuel had already seen what Moses saw?

TCG: Much further.

The Thirty-Seventh Message - Moses' purpose – dying?

TCG: Did you notice something different about Moses?

Enoch: What do you mean?

TCG: *"The LORD thy God will raise up unto thee a Prophet from the midst of thee, of thy brethren, like unto me; unto him ye shall hearken; According to all that thou desiredst of the LORD thy God in Horeb in the day of the assembly, saying, Let me not hear again the voice of the LORD my God, neither let me see this great fire any more, that I die not."* (Deuteronomy 18, 15-16)

Enoch: I remember this; Moses was speaking of a False Prophet.

TCG: And Moses stated two things about such a person who is condemned to die:

   a. A person who commands things not commanded by God.
   b. A person who speaks to the people with the words of other gods.

Enoch: I do not think I follow your logic.

TCG: Why did Moses die?

Enoch: What are you saying?!

TCG: What were we talking about?

Enoch: A prophet that died.

TCG: And which prophet might that be?

Enoch: I know that you are expecting me to say "Moses".

TCG: A person who would harm the covenant between God and the Israelites, would be condemned to die: *"And thou shalt do according to the* *sentence, which they of that place which the* LORD *shall choose shall shew thee; and thou shalt observe to do according to all that they inform thee...thou shalt not decline from the sentence which they shall shew thee, to the right hand, nor to the left. And the man that will do presumptuously, and will not hearken unto the priest that standeth to minister there before the* LORD *thy God, or unto the judge, even that man shall die: and thou shalt put away the evil from Israel."* (Deuteronomy 17, 10-12)

<u>Enoch:</u> I do not think I follow: who was Moses talking about?

<u>TCG:</u> He was talking about the people; after he received the effect he wishes for, he also added: *"And all the people shall hear, and fear, and do no more presumptuously."* (Deuteronomy 17, 13) But was Moses speaking about the people or <u>himself?</u>

<u>Enoch:</u> How can you say that?

<u>TCG:</u> Did Moses tell and command the people what he was commanded by God? Did he not speak the truth? Is it not true that for his transgressions against the people by accusing them of certain incidents, he was sent to his death?

<u>Enoch:</u> You would need to be a lot more specific.

<u>TCG:</u> After the spies returned, did he not accuse the Israelites of forcing him to send spies to Canaan, even though he did this completely at his own volition after God had told him to only send emissaries?

<u>Enoch:</u> So you are saying he brought this unto himself? That he <u>deserved to die?</u>

<u>TCG:</u> I am asking you; do you have an answer for that? If so, say it.

<u>Enoch:</u> And you do not find this accusation extreme?

TCG: I am not accusing anyone of anything, I am just quoting the scriptures. Moses could not ask the people to do what he was not willing to do. But, this is but a metaphor.

Enoch: I would need to think about this.

The Thirty-Eighth Message - The Usual Suspect

TCG: Enoch, you must first understand that my answers are not mine alone – I am but the messenger here to educate you.

Enoch: And who am I in this equation, the prophet? Hehe.

TCG: You are "the vessel" in which I may pour this knowledge of this calling.

Enoch: "Vessel for a calling"? No thanks.

TCG: I am a guide and you are the vessel in my calling, and when you find it difficult for understanding, I must find the answer to your questions.

Enoch: In Moses' death, God has already promised Moses that he would not enter Canaan. He would die on top of the mountain – how so?

TCG: You will be the judge of that, this is a tad tricky.

Enoch: Exactly what I expected to hear. I would like you to speak about all the different factors and considerations God had in this decision.

TCG: Do you remember the Meribah Sin? We spoke about this, the people demanded water and Moses hit the rock with his cane. He hit it instead of speaking to it, as he was commanded to do.

Enoch: Yes, I remember that; it was quite juvenile in my opinion to punish him for that.

TCG: One might write it off as such, but there is a lot more to it than that which made God decide that Moses would not be the one to lead the Israelites into The Promised Land. We spoke about the fact that hitting the rock, instead of speaking to it has generated a punishment for Moses. But it is not the only reason why he was punished for it, but the way he spoke unto the people saying it which drew God to the conclusion that Moses was no longer the man for the job: *"Hear now, ye rebels; must we fetch you water out of this rock?"* (Numbers 20, 10) What kind of a leader calls his people "rebels"? Moses was deflecting the blame from him unto the people. The following massacre at Meribah ("Waters of Strife") has but only one person to be blamed for, Moses. But that was not the only reason for it. God intended

Moses to speak to the rock, so the people <u>would witness the awesome power of God</u>. Moses did not give any credit to God, which is why he was no longer the chosen one in his eyes to lead these people into Canaan.

Enoch: What is your proof for this?

TCG: Two referenced sources:

1. *"And the Lord spake unto Moses and Aaron, Because ye believed me not, to sanctify me in the eyes of the children of Israel, therefore ye shall not bring this congregation into the land which I have given them."* (Numbers 20, 12) Which means that the Israelites shamed God and did not give him the credit he was so deserved, as if the Israelites were the ones to generate that miracle.

2. *"They angered him also at the waters of strife, so that it went ill with Moses for their sakes: Because they provoked his spirit, so that he spake unadvisedly with his lips."* (Psalm 106, 32-33) Even David who wrote the Book of Psalms, knew that the Israelites gave no credit to God for granting water of thin air. This is exactly why Moses was forbidden from entering Canaan.

Enoch: And then we know what happened with the spies, to seal the deal here.

TCG: Precisely so. God told Moses to send people to tour the land, but he decided to send people **to spy on the land**. Moses did not trust God well enough to tell the people that God would deliver them, the same way he delivered them from Egypt and the wilderness.

Enoch: That I understand, but why are we still at this?

TCG: Deuteronomy opens with the fact that Moses knew God had blamed him for what happened with the spies; it was his ministerial and leading responsibility. It happened in his watch.

Enoch: So Moses was twice denied entry to Canaan?

TCG: No, he was once denied to lead the people into Canaan and the second time around, he was denied entry to Canaan as well due to what happened at Meribah and with the spies.

Enoch: Which is why he was to die?

The Thirty-Ninth Message - Stoning of the boys

TCG: I know what you are thinking Enoch, but these laws are Moses' – not God's.

Enoch: But why would he even make these up?

TCG: These laws were quite common among the people living around the Israelites. Moses only tried to amend them to the divine moral compass of God.

Enoch: The last thing you could say about these laws is that they were "moral".

TCG: Moses spoke about the Rules of War and the treatment of Prisoners of War, and then moved sharply towards the morality of war. Moses humanly saw this, but not in terms of "compassion".

Enoch: So the compensation for the liberator of The Promised Land is either gold or a woman?

TCG: Do these rules make any sense to you, Enoch? Do they sound reasonable to your ears?

Enoch: Laws of the Jungle. Brutality everywhere you go.

TCG: No, this is what <u>Moses wants</u>. He wants to ensure that "moral" makes sense, to appease God in his eyes: *"If a man have two wives, one beloved, and another hated, and they have born him children, both the beloved and the hated; and if the firstborn son be hers that was hated: Then it shall be, when he maketh his sons to inherit that which he hath, that he may not make the son of the beloved firstborn before the son of the hated, which is indeed the firstborn."* (Deuteronomy 21, 15-16) Even if the firstborn is the one of the hated wife, he still is the firstborn and he inherits the lot of it.

Enoch: Only Moses could be this cruel, no emotion: who cares whose child it was? It was that man's child as well. Why could that man not send that hated wife away? How could a person even conceive a child with a hated woman? Why would he do this? These sound like the ramblings of an old man, not the Moses we have known before.

TCG: I think you won the game; well done, Enoch. Moses was 120 years old, an old and weary man. This moral compass of his was completely off course, which is why a rational and decent man would never even consider such a law to be the right way to treat one's sons.

Enoch: What could he possibly make up next?

TCG: What do you think of this: *"If a man have a stubborn and rebellious son...Then shall his father and his mother lay hold on him, and bring him out unto the elders of his city, and unto the gate of his place; And they shall say unto the elders of his city, This our son is stubborn and rebellious, he will not obey our voice; he is a glutton, and a drunkard. And all the men of his city shall stone him with stones, that he die: so shalt thou put evil away from among you."* (Deuteronomy 21, 18-21) This is what Moses believes the people should do to their sons. Grab the child, beat the child and kill it outside of the city walls.

Enoch: So much for education.

TCG: Up until that point, everything Moses said was given as granted. Now, even the author of the book was appalled by this and wrote the following: *"and all Israel shall hear, and fear."* Moses did not notice that, but the people lost their trust in him at that point. He lost the people's support of his actions.

Enoch: Such a crude individual.

The Fortieth Message - Moses the Merciful(?)

TCG: Moses was trying to repair his image in the eyes of the people (and God). He may have genuinely thought about doing that, even though he did not say it out loud.

Enoch: What did he say?

TCG: Sending away the nest for example.

Enoch: Morality and sensitivity, things we have never seen before in Moses. The basic rights of animals.

TCG: He naturally first gave precedence to food, as the basis of life. But, even though some laws sound moral, they are not moral laws, such as not boiling a kid (goat) in its mother's milk.

Enoch: I still do not understand this law.

TCG: The Israelites were forbidden from eating cadavers, nor boiling kids in their mother's milk not because it was immoral, but because it was something the gentiles around them practised, probably for religious fertility reasons. The reason is that *"thou art an holy people unto the LORD thy God"* (Deuteronomy 14, 21) But it also states that the Israelites may give these to the gentiles living by their city gates, as Moses knew that they consume cadavers as part of their diet.

Enoch: So the Israelites would only kill an animal to eat it, yes?

TCG: Bravo!

Enoch: So how is it that the ancients, in their interpretation of the Pentateuch, decided that eating any kind of meat with milk is forbidden?

TCG: It does not matter what they thought or interpreted; you have the book laid in front of you, you know to read it aloud to yourself and you have a sharp mind with which you may analyse what is written and make your own mind. They interpreted what they interpreted as they were not aware of any gentiles doing something similar around them. The world changed in between living in the wilderness in the 13th Century BC, and what the ancients had interpreted over a millennium later.

Enoch: And what about the bird and the eggs?

TCG: Giving thanks to the bounty God has given unto the Israelites; they may not cut down trees with birds on them, as the birds dwell there – they cannot just decide that those birds must leave, especially if they are nesting. Hence, they should first send out the nest and only then could they decide if the tree must be cut. There is life in everything, and the Israelites as a holy people must know and adhere to that.

The Forty-First Message - Ruth and Deuteronomy

Enoch: It appears Moses has a strong attraction towards rules involving mixed-breeds, fabrics or the role of men or women in relationships. Do you mind if we dwell on this for a while?

TCG: What contradictions are you looking for? Should a man engage in sexual relations with a married woman, he and she would be put to death. The same goes for a man who finds an engaged woman. Despite the option of a woman giving her consent to sexual congress with that man, we understand where these commandments stem from - the purity of the family and the woman.

Enoch: The purity of the family and the woman?

TCG: We both know Moses was socially awkward and knew nothing about relationships or love for that matter, hence why this warped sense of understanding in such relationships.

Enoch: What are you saying?

TCG: In his eyes, and according to what was considered "acceptable" in those days, a woman would rather be married to her rapist and not stay alone for the rest of her life, than be happy alone. It was expected of every woman to marry, which is why the rapist had to pay a fine to the father of the raped woman and had to marry her and stay with her till the rest of their natural lives.

Enoch: This is how you treat an animal, not a person.

TCG: This is the flaw in Moses' understanding of Man. This is how women were treated in the Near East 33 centuries ago. You cannot see this in your eyes but their eyes. You cannot forget that Moses sent away his own wife and children; they have never been mentioned again, which means that he was an awful father and a husband, which is ironic considering his position as the father of the nation.

Enoch: I too find this odd.

TCG: But let us stumble upon something more important: *"An Ammonite or Moabite shall not enter into the congregation of the LORD; even to their tenth generation shall they not enter into the congregation of the LORD for ever: Because they met you not with bread and with water in the way, when ye came forth out of Egypt; and because they hired against thee Balaam the son of Beor of Pethor of Mesopotamia, to curse thee...Thou shalt not seek their peace nor their prosperity all thy days for ever. Thou shalt not abhor an Edomite; for he is thy brother: thou shalt not abhor an Egyptian; because thou wast a stranger in his land."* (Deuteronomy 23, 3-7) The Israelites would not accept any strangers into their midst, even if they would dwell there for 250 years.

Enoch: Does not seem to be any different than most places around the globe; xenophobia is not a novel idea.

TCG: God always sees into the future and creates a way in between the times, it is never some rift in time which cannot be explained.

Enoch: And how is that a bad thing?

TCG: Let us speak about Elimelech who left Bethlehem to live in the fields of Moab.

Enoch: Well, we know it was illegal as the Israelites were not supposed to have any relations with the Moabites.

TCG: Yes, he has betrayed the land by leaving it and immigrating to Moab, which was a sworn enemy of Israel at the time. His sons were married to two Moabite women, how so? These women cannot be married to nor can they be converted to become Israelites. The sons die and Ruth, one of his daughters in law, decided to stay with Naomi saying: *"Intreat me not to leave thee, or to return from following after thee: for whither thou goest, I will go; and where thou lodgest, I will lodge: thy people shall be my people, and thy God my God."*

(Ruth 1, 16) Ruth does not know she cannot join the Israelites? And then we learn about the fact that Ruth later married Boaz, who was no other than King David's great-grandfather. So we know this conversion did not really happen since it was forbidden.

Enoch: And the author did not know that fact?

TCG: He did know that, but he wanted to make a political statement. This book was found after Ezra demanded that all foreign women and the children born to them with Jewish men would be sent away in the 6th century when the Jews built the Second Temple in Jerusalem. He had to make Boaz and Ruth's marriage legitimate, otherwise, he could not demand any man to send his wife and children away. So all foreign women were then converted to avoid a possible crisis of faith, let alone a civil war.

Enoch: So much for doing what is written in the book.

TCG: And now that you are thinking about it, did God forbid the Israelites from coming near the Moabites or was it Moses...?

The Forty-Second Message - Deus Ex Machina

Enoch: I am trying to figure out whom you represent; who are you protecting?

TCG: The truth in The Scriptures. Whether it be directly from God or Moses' interpretation – makes little difference to me. I am giving you both realms to choose from.

Enoch: So you explain to me and my audience about the divine way, which is what Moses was trying to relay to us all.

TCG: Yes, but what matters is what the audience in those days thought about Moses' way of interpretation, was it possible to follow all these rules and if so – at what cost? Would the Israelites be coerced to follow these rules or their understanding of those rules is what made them follow the rules in the first place?

Enoch: I understand.

TCG: Let us continue with the rules of morality by Moses: *"A man shall not take his father's wife, nor discover his father's skirt."* (Deuteronomy 22, 30) The first part makes sense, what about the second one?

Enoch: So the son may not shame his father?

TCG: Precisely; this is exactly what Ham had done unto his father, Noah: *"And Ham...saw the nakedness of his father, and told his two brethren without. And Shem and Japheth took a garment, and laid it upon both their shoulders, and went backward...and their faces were backward, and they saw not their father's nakedness."* (Genesis 9, 22-23) So we know that Ham already knew what was about to happen, while his brothers honoured their father by covering him and not taking any glimpse at his naked state, which is why Ham was then punished – through his son, Canaan.

Enoch: But how does that correspond with what Moses said: *"The fathers shall not be put to death for the children, neither shall the children be put to death for the fathers: every man shall be put to death for his own sin."* (Deuteronomy 24, 16)

TCG: Yes, Moses did say so but the sons always pay for the sins of their fathers, as Noah said to Ham: *"And he said, Cursed be Canaan; a servant of servants shall he be unto his brethren."* (Genesis 9, 25) So who here is against the injustice – Moses or God? Moses also spoke about the Edomites and that they should not be hated. Why did it matter? Because the Edomites <u>are the sons of Esau and Ishmael</u>, which means they too are worthy of God's blessing to Abraham at the covenant. That is why we understand why some of the people in the area were hated and others were accepted into the congregation: *"Thou shalt not abhor an Edomite; for he is thy brother: thou shalt not abhor an Egyptian; because thou wast a stranger in his land."* (Deuteronomy 23, 7)

Enoch: But how can they be "brothers"?

TCG: *"The children that are begotten of them shall enter into the congregation of the LORD in their third generation."* (Deuteronomy 23, 9) These people are more "pure" than the rest, hence by the third generation (the grandchildren born within the borders of the Israelites' cities), they may be accepted into the Israelite, as they are brothers.

Enoch: I still do not see how that is possible.

TCG: Contrary to the conversion regulations of today, both the Edomites and the Egyptians were able to join the Israelites; John Hyrcanus, the Hasmonean leader of the 2nd century BCE, force converted the Idumeans (Edomites) into the Jewish faith for they were genetically related to the Judeans (Jews). Esau (leader and ancestor of the Edomites) was Jacob's brother (his twin brother) who married his half-cousin Bosmat, daughter of his half-uncle, Ishmael (half-brother to Isaac), hence the blood tie to Israelites was strong between the Edomites and the Israelites. You can never forget the most prominent figure of this kind of conversion: Herod the Great, whose father was Edomite and grew up a Jew and became the King of Judea during the Roman era.

Enoch: I see other interesting rules, especially about vows.

TCG: *"When thou shalt vow a vow unto the Lord thy God, thou shalt not slack to pay it: for the Lord thy God will surely require it of thee; and it would be sin in thee."* (Deuteronomy 23, 21)

Enoch: So vows must be fulfilled and kept?

TCG: Yes, with tragedies arising when Jephthah the judge fought the Ammonites and vowed *"Then it shall be, that whatsoever cometh forth of the doors of my house to meet me, when I return in peace from the children of Ammon, shall surely be the Lord's, and I will offer it up for a burnt offering."* (Judges 11, 31)

Enoch: And who eventually came out of that house, I do not remember?

TCG: His daughter with her maidens, dancing and holding the tambourine, celebrating her father's victory and his glorious return home.

Enoch: So he did win the battle? But seriously, that is not a proper example of faith.

TCG: That is most probably the most extreme example of the vows which men take upon themselves to keep.

Enoch: So, did he actually fulfil his vow? He sacrificed his own daughter as Agamemnon did in the Illiad?

TCG: Since human sacrifice is taboo in the Israelite (and today's Jewish) faith, Jephathah's punishment was to see his daughter come out first of the house. That is why money could be given in exchange for the sacrifice; a rudimentary explanation of the term "blood money", at least in those days. That is the first commandment Moses has devised that have made such a tragedy possible.

Enoch: So Jephathah could not break his vow?

TCG: According to The Scriptures, he did not even try to. He just tore his clothes as is customary when mourning and told his daughter that he cannot break his vow.

Enoch: Reminds me of The Bindinf of Isaac.

TCG: Very similar, you are right.

Enoch: So what may one surmise from this?

TCG: Vows must be kept, hence people should try and not take one unto themselves in the first place.

The Forty-Third Message - The Amalekites (and Leprosy)

TCG: You think you know everything about the commandments, which is why you want to move forward as fast as possible. But let us understand the basic moral perception of people those days, which has become the standard practice of manners and etiquette in the modern era, such as this: *"Take heed in the plague of leprosy, that thou observe diligently, and do according to all that the priests the Levites shall teach you: as I commanded them, so ye shall observe to do."* (Deuteronomy 24, 8)

Enoch: Taking caution and staying back from the plague, that is reasonable.

TCG: You are missing the subtleties here.

Enoch: Well, the priests' role is obscure. What was Moses up to?

TCG: *"Remember what the Lord thy God did unto Miriam by the way, after that ye were come forth out of Egypt."* (Deuteronomy 24, 9)

Enoch: So he was talking about the divine retribution inflicted upon his sister, Miriam. It had nothing to do with the plague, but using fear to control the people via the Levites and priests.

TCG: Miriam was inflicted with leprosy because of her jealously of Moses, while Moses thought that leprosy was a punishment administered to the ones who do not obey. It was unlike any other plague at the time.

Enoch: It sure did not sound like the voice of God.

TCG: And here is another commandment which must be followed: *"Remember what Amalek did unto thee by the way, when ye were come forth out of Egypt."* (Deuteronomy 25, 17)

Enoch: Amalek is everywhere in the Old Testament.

TCG: *"How he met thee by the way, and smote the hindmost of thee, even all that were feeble behind thee, when thou wast faint and weary; and he feared not God."* (Deuteronomy 25, 18)

Enoch: What is the point of saying that, to make the Israelites hate them more?

TCG: "United we stand, divided we fall" – Aesop; Amalek was the one arch-nemesis of Israel which must be eradicated.

Enoch: That I understand that they were wretch, but still – why them?

TCG: Every nation must have a common enemy to keep itself united at all costs; for the Israelites, it was Amalek. Therefore Moses has also added this verse: *"Therefore it shall be, when the LORD thy God hath given thee rest from all thine enemies round about, in the land which the LORD thy God giveth thee for an inheritance to possess it, that thou shalt blot out the remembrance of Amalek from under heaven; thou shalt not forget it."* (Deuteronomy 25, 19)

Enoch: I am trying to wrap my head around this; I mean, Amalek has been mentioned more than once in the Old Testament and on many occasions. Were there any dividing conflicts which have arisen from this commandment?

TCG: I did not wish to delve into that, but since you brought it up I had to ask more. In the future of the Israelites in Canaan, we find that this commandment and promise to eradicate Amalek has put a wedge between the priesthood and the monarchy. The young King Saul had an altercation with the old prophet, Samuel. This is where religion and government clash with one another. Samuel tried to submit Saul to his will, demanding that Saul keep his promise of eradicating Amalek after his victory over the Ammonites and Philistines. Samuel had demanded Saul to partake in another lengthy war which had no provocation with the Amalekites, solely based on the ancient "curse" for the Amalekites: to be eradicated as they may jeopardise the future of the Israelites.

Saul spared the life of Agag, king of the Amalekites, as well as his herds – but that is because his men demanded him to do so. It is conceivable that Saul took pity on them and was easily influenced. He already spared the Kenites (who were within the realm of the Amalekites): *"And Saul said unto the Kenites, Go, depart, get you down from among the Amalekites, lest I destroy you*

with them: for ye shewed kindness to all the children of Israel, when they came up out
of Egypt...And Saul smote the Amalekites from Havilah...And he took Agag the king
of the Amalekites alive, and utterly destroyed all the people with the edge of the
sword. But Saul and the people spared Agag, and the best of the sheep...and all that
was good, and would not utterly destroy them...

And Samuel said, Hath the Lord *as great delight in burnt offerings and sacrifices, as*
in obeying the voice of the Lord*...Because thou hast rejected the word of the* Lord*, he*
hath also rejected thee from being king. And Saul said unto Samuel, I have sinned:
for I have transgressed the commandment of the Lord*, and thy words...*

And Samuel said unto Saul...and the Lord *hath rejected thee from being king over*
Israel. And as Samuel turned about to go away, he laid hold upon the skirt of his
mantle, and it rent. And Samuel said unto him, The Lord *hath rent the kingdom of*
Israel from thee this day, and hath given it to a neighbour of thine, that is better than
thou..." (1 Samuel 15, 6-29) Saul did not even want to become king; Samuel
anointed him three times before he accepted his calling to be the king of
Israel. This is how, eventually, David became the king of Israel in his stead.

Enoch: So all of this happened to Saul, the first king of Israel, just because of
that sworn auth to destroy Amalek, even if fighting them does not
jeopardise Israel?

TCG: As I mentioned before – the arch-nemesis. Whether or not Amalek
jeopardises Israel, it should be destroyed.

Enoch: And that is the tragic tale of Saul.

TCG: Yes; despite eradicating paganism and killing of idol priests, the crown
was taken away from him.

Enoch: So how come God did not accept his repentance?

<u>**TCG:**</u> The Dogma of God's words:

1. All commandments must be obeyed
2. To make an example of Saul for future generations
3. Religion is always above the monarchy – the longest of disputes in history

The Forty-Fourth Message - Dethroned but still giving orders

TCG: Are the divine commandments based on Moses' understanding or did Moses try to make rules for the future and religion part of people's lives?

Enoch: What are you implying?

TCG: Moses took upon himself the role of God; not on a sinister note or that he wished his voice to be heard instead of God's, but as to complement God's voice.

Enoch: Sounds like a Third Act Twist, this is not what you first taught us.

TCG: I find it as silly as when the sons of Aaron tried to worship God out of a sense of obligation, though they were never obligated to do so.

Enoch: So they were punished by being burnt for having initiative?

TCG: God does not appreciate these "initiatives" which do not correspond with the instructions given within his commandments. He conveyed a "hard" message so people would understand it.

Enoch: But to take a life? Is it not excessive?

TCG: Your repeated hybris is that you judge God with human eyes; God does not see it the same way as Man. Sacrificing others for "the greater good" is preferable.

Enoch: Means to an end?

TCG: We need to first understand how God has created the world and every living thing in it lives in perfect harmony with other living things. Once we understand that, we would not lose our way. We must first be able to read between the lines and understand how punishments the ancients received are similar to punishments we receive today and what is the purpose of these punishments.

Enoch: Such as with Covid19?

TCG: Precisely; God had given the gift of vaccination and immune system to people if they all work together.

Enoch: Cause and effect. I think I understand it now more than ever.

TCG: Once we can understand that we must accept the good with the bad, we would be able to comprehend God's plan. Let us continue: *"When men strive together one with another, and the wife of the one draweth near for to deliver her husband out of the hand of him that smiteth him, and putteth forth her hand, and taketh him by the secrets: Then thou shalt cut off her hand, thine eye shall not pity her."* (Deuteronomy 25, 11-12) We understand that women in those times went for "the jewels", otherwise Moses would take no notice for this. We understand that women did this to save their husbands and this has nothing to do with humility or chastity.

Enoch: So what is the problem? That a woman may not hold unto another man's "jewels"?

TCG: Yes, should she does hold unto those, her hand must be cut off – does that sound to you like something God would command people to do?

Enoch: Yes, but what wrong could she have caused to constitute such punishment? Is it possible that Moses was no more than a misogynist?

TCG: Moses' intention was not about the criminal "offence" but a symbolic one, which is the emasculation of another man. In his eyes, this kind of action degrades the man by a woman and at the same time, threatens his ability to reproduce – which is too, symbolic.

Enoch: That is preposterous; so a degraded man should have a woman's hand cut off?! Ridiculous!

TCG: That is the law, a commandment concocted by Moses. Moses tried to make this rule into law so that people would have rules to live by.

Enoch: He did not trust Joshua then.

The Forty-Fifth Message - Moses the Patriot

Enoch: Was Moses the first patriot in Jewish history?

TCG: It appears so; he craved so much to live in the land of his ancestor, and despite his shortcomings – he still wanted to be the shepherd leading the herd back home. In his eyes, the people were stubborn and rebellious, but he still wanted to lead them.

Enoch: You told me that God was the one who chose the Israelites as his people, not the other way around. You mentioned that these enslaved people never prayed to God to save them from the Egyptians, but this was God's initiative to do so.

TCG: That is true, God waited for the right time "to recruit" Moses for this mission. The new pharaoh was a rookie and it would be easier to persuade him because Moses grew up in his house and knew everything about the Egyptian regime at firm hand.

Enoch: But Moses had already found refuge with Jethro, he had a wife and son already.

TCG: You need to understand something, Enoch: "Jethro" is but a title of the high priest of Median; the name of the person was Reuel. This was a marriage of comfort for Moses, not of love. Despite having two sons with Zipporah, Moses cared not for their well-being and they are never mentioned again.

Enoch: And what about the Israelites? How was it that their cry was heard by God?

TCG: Why do you think that was? How is it that their cry was heard only after the evil king died, the same one who killed their babies – the same one who pursued Moses? This was the time for God "to shine". To deliver his people from Egypt while punishing Pharaoh severely. These acts of cunning and leadership would then persuade the Israelites to leave Egypt for a better future of bounty. That was the divine calling – the delivering of the

Hebrews out of Egypt. God had concocted this plan at the perfect timing for him.

Enoch: How so? Why now?

TCG: This is when the people were aware of God's crafty plans.

Enoch: Do tell.

TCG: Pharaoh was dead and only now was God able to hear the cries of the Israelites; he then took Moses, his chosen prophet, and taught him all of his magic to persuade the Israelites to leave Egypt and coerce Pharaoh himself to let them go, while taking his vengeance upon him for everyone to see. And here was Moses, free of this binding by taking refuge in Median.

Enoch: What is the big secret then? How is that relevant to what Moses said in Deuteronomy?

TCG: Closure; Moses was speaking about the Israelites and his role in saving them saying: *"And thou shalt speak and say before the LORD thy God, A Syrian ready to perish was my father, and he went down into Egypt...And the Egyptians evil entreated us...And when we cried unto the LORD God of our fathers, the LORD heard our voice...And the LORD brought us forth out of Egypt with a mighty hand, and with an outstretched arm...And he hath brought us into this place, and hath given us this land, even a land that floweth with milk and honey."* (Deuteronomy 26, 5-9)

Enoch: But you said that was not correct; the Israelites never cried for God to deliver them; they were crying for years and only now did God plead with their cry. Is that correct?

TCG: Yes, but up until that moment it was <u>not the right time for them</u>: *"And thou shalt rejoice in every good thing which the LORD thy God hath given unto thee, and unto thine house, thou, and the Levite, and the stranger that is among you."* (Deuteronomy 26, 11) It was now the time to enter The Promised Land. Here

Moses was promising the Israelites all of this bounty, and what did they need to do in return?

Enoch: Follow God's and Moses' commandments?

TCG: Precisely.

The Forty-Sixth Message - The Elders' Support

TCG: I would like to share with you one of the core pillars of Judaism, which has become in some ways part of other Abrahamic religions such as Christianity or Islam. I would like you to think to whom Moses has given the "Oral Torah", which some denominations reject entirely.

Enoch: Interesting.

TCG: You need to understand for yourself things from within the verses themselves: *"And Moses with the elders of Israel commanded the people, saying, Keep all the commandments which I command you this day."* (Deuteronomy 27, 1)

Enoch: I fail to see the difference; the entire book is written like that.

TCG: Wrong. We always read about Moses' instructions to his people, but this time the elders have joined him. These wise men held public positions, where they were able to even judge individuals according to Mosaic Law.

Enoch: Fine, what are you trying to prove then?

TCG: Their authority under God's divine law, and what would happen to the ones who disobey the elders? They would die. The people were afraid of Moses' threats.

Enoch: That we already know from Deuteronomy 17, what is the difference?

TCG: Moses only spoke and commanded – here he let the wisemen help him.

Enoch: It makes sense; they were his aides delivering judgement.

TCG: And that was their only purpose or did they also see the future the same way he has?

Enoch: The elders support Moses – what is the clue that you were trying to convey to me?

TCG: Where was his successor at that time?

Enoch: Joshua? He was not dealing with education and teachings.

TCG: What was he doing then? He was not even chosen by Moses to stand beside him and receive the legitimacy as his successor, to be "the guide" of the people, let alone the "prophet" as he lacked that skill set.

Enoch: Was it not his job to lead the Israelites into Canaan?

TCG: Moses has never chosen Joshua as his successor. It was God who had chosen Joshua. Moses wanted to continue leading the Israelites into The Promised Land. He believed that he deserved to do so after doing so much for the people. At that moment, Moses was able to prove to everyone that he was their saviour, being backed by the elders unanimously. All influential men took part in this act. Joshua was nowhere to be found. Joshua was also not speaking at any given moment.

Enoch: And?

TCG: You will see soon enough.

The Forty-Seventh Message - More about the Oral Torah

Enoch: I read that in some of the Mishnaic scriptures, it is said to whom God's law was passed by Moses.

TCG: Fine, who do you think Moses passed the law to?

Enoch: To Joshua, who in turn passed it to the elders.

TCG: And who gave the order to do so, Moses? Did he decide this on his own or was he instructed to do this? Where do you see that written?

Enoch: It is considered fact.

TCG: Are we speaking about the same set of laws?

Enoch: In Deuteronomy, that is the written law while Moses passed the oral law to others.

TCG: And what is the oral law? How does it differ from the written one?

Enoch: The oral one is also God's law.

TCG: God had given Moses two sets of laws? Are you certain? **One Oral** and another written? Because Moses wrote an entirely different account of what you are saying: *"...and all the people answered with one voice, and said, All the words which the LORD hath said will we do."* (Exodus 24, 3) But then Moses wrote it in a book which is called "The Book of the Covenant": *"And he declared unto you his covenant, which he commanded you to perform, even ten commandments; and he wrote them upon two tables of stone."* (Deuteronomy 4, 13) So even Moses says there were only two tablets.

Enoch: Where is that written?

TCG: Deuteronomy 4, 4-9; Moses had said so himself.

Enoch: And again, that is the written one – it is well-known that Moses received another one, an oral one – secrets which could not be written.

TCG: And where is that written? Even Moses says that there were only the tablets on which the Ten Commandments were written.

Enoch: That is how he claimed.

TCG: *"And he gave unto Moses, when he had made an end of communing with him upon mount Sinai, two tables of testimony, tables of stone, written with the finger of God."* (Exodus 31, 18) Only the stone tablets which are the written testimony by Moses.

Enoch: Well, that is how the ancients interpreted.

TCG: The odds of finding literate people among a nation which was enslaved for over 400 years are slim to none. Not only that but the fact that they were able to find both parchments (which means they had people who knew how to make such material) as well as writing tools when the only person who knew how to write was Moses, who most probably did not know Hebrew writing but Egyptian writing, were slim to none. The only other people in the vicinity who knew how to write on parchment (or papyrus for that matter) were too far away and without ties to Israel, which would make this assumption implausible. The only person who could have written this was Moses, who grew up in Pharaoh's household, an Egyptian prince who knew how to read and write Egyptian, was well-versed in the arts of war and applied jurisprudence and more. Do you honestly believe Joshua, the son of slaves, was literate? We already know that Joshua waited on Moses; Moses never asked him to help him carry the tablets which were made of stone? It is also said that Moses broke the first tablets, was the stone that thin? Was it thick? Did Joshua even understand what he saw on the stone?

Enoch: I suppose not.

TCG: You need to understand something: if anything appears to you as illogical, it most probably is and may have never happened.

Enoch: What are you implying?

TCG: The Oral Torah could not have been written in Moses' time, as much as it could not have happened before his time.

Enoch: What are you saying?

TCG: The Written Torah and the Oral Torah <u>are the same</u>. Naturally, it is not the same "Oral Torah" you are referring to, but it was given orally. Generations of leaders and priests were able to make the people believe more in God and his Commandments via oral tradition, as most of the people were illiterate.

Enoch: I never saw it this way.

TCG: Illiterate people must recite, otherwise they will forget. They do not have the luxury of literate people, able to reread certain laws themselves.

Enoch: it is hard for me to fathom this.

TCG: I know, but I will prove it more to you when the time comes.

The Forty-Eighth Message - Moses commissions the written law

TCG: Let us review what has happened: The Israelites were on the brink of Canaan, The Promised Land, and still not everything was clear to them. Moses as their guide had needed to add commandments and help them complete what was missing so the people could have laws to live by.

Enoch: And these are the laws of God?

TCG: Some of them are; some were Moses' interpretations of God's laws which were simplified for the people to understand. You must not forget there were laws given by Moses and Aaron which God had never uttered, and what would God have said in return? Nothing.

Enoch: So Moses was a teacher.

TCG: He was; he wanted people to behave in the way he perceived God would prefer.

Enoch: And this miraculous initiative was not enough for God to turn his decree?

TCG: God sees the big picture, hence why he could not spare Moses. But we are digressing here: *"Therefore it shall be when ye be gone over Jordan, that ye shall set up these stones, which I command you this day, in mount Ebal, and thou shalt plaister them with plaister. And there shalt thou build an altar unto the LORD thy God, an altar of stones...and thou shalt offer burnt offerings thereon unto the LORD thy God: And thou shalt offer peace offerings, and shalt eat there, and rejoice before the LORD thy God. And thou shalt write upon the stones all the words of this law very plainly. These are the words of the covenant, which the LORD commanded Moses to make with the children of Israel in the land of Moab, beside the covenant which he made with them in Horeb...And I have led you forty years in the wilderness: your clothes are not waxen old upon you, and thy shoe is not waxen old upon thy foot...that ye might know that I am the LORD your God. And* *when ye came unto this place, Sihon the king of Heshbon, and Og the king of Bashan, came out against us unto battle, and we smote them....And Moses went and spake these words unto all Israel. And he said unto them, I am an hundred and twenty years old this day; I can no more go out and come in: also the* Lord *hath said unto me, Thou shalt not go over this Jordan. The* Lord *thy God, he will go over before thee, and he will destroy these nations from before thee, and thou shalt possess them: and Joshua, he shall go over before thee, as the* Lord *hath said."* (Deuteronomy 27, 4-8, 29, 1-8, 31, 1-3) So the people now know that Moses would not be crossing the Jordan with them into The Promised Land; we know that Moses was now finally addressing Joshua as his successor and told the Israelites to write everything on stones so it would stay forever.

Enoch: So Moses was retiring?

TCG: More like staying on the bylines than anything. So you see, the Oral Torah was now the written one on stones, it was not over just yet.

The Forty-Ninth Message - What of the people?

TCG: We now know that Moses made peace with his fate and continued with the people towards a certain point in the Jordan from which he may not pass and finally recognized Joshua as his successor: *"The LORD thy God, he will go over before thee, and he will destroy these nations from before thee...and Joshua, he shall go over before thee, as the LORD hath said...And the LORD shall give them up before your face, that ye may do unto them according unto all the commandments which I have commanded you...for the LORD thy God, he it is that doth go with thee; he will not fail thee, nor forsake thee. And Moses called unto Joshua, and said unto him in the sight of all Israel, Be strong and of a good courage: for thou must go with this people unto the land which the LORD hath sworn unto their fathers to give them; and thou shalt cause them to inherit it. And the LORD, he it is that doth go before thee; he will be with thee, he will not fail thee, neither forsake thee: fear not, neither be dismayed."* (Deuteronomy 31, 3-8) So Moses was finally coming to terms with the fact that Joshua was his successor, he would be leading the people into Canaan, smite the enemies of the Israelites and creating a strong nation in the area.

Enoch: It seems to me that now Moses wished to be Joshua's mentor and bless him a moment before dying and naturally – never entering Canaan.

TCG: He was also blessing the Israelites and telling the Levites to put the teaching on paper and stone, so the people may not forget the laws and commandments of God. Not only that but they were commanded to read to the people from the commandments on the seventh year, on the Feast of Tabernacles (Sukkot).

Enoch: And where did that take place?

TCG: *"And Moses wrote this law, and delivered it unto the priests the sons of Levi, which bare the ark of the covenant of the Lord, and unto all the elders of Israel. ...When all Israel is come to appear before the Lord thy God in the place which he shall choose, thou shalt read this law before all Israel in their hearing. Gather the people together, men and women, and children, and thy stranger that is within thy gates, that they may hear, and that they may learn, and fear the Lord your God, and observe to do all the words of this law: And that their children, which have not known any thing, may hear, and learn to fear the Lord your God, as long as ye live in the land whither ye go over Jordan to possess it."* (Deuteronomy 31, 9-13) This is not unlike what Ezra and Nehemiah had done about eight centuries later, building the Second Temple in Jerusalem.

Enoch: It is almost poetic.

TCG: And this was Moses' blessing (and a warning) for Joshua: *"And the Lord said unto Moses, Behold, thy days approach that thou must die: call Joshua, and present yourselves in the tabernacle of the congregation, that I may give him a charge. And Moses and Joshua went, and presented themselves in the tabernacle of the congregation...And the Lord said unto Moses, Behold, thou shalt sleep with thy fathers; and this people will rise up, and go a whoring after the gods of the strangers of the land, whither they go to be among them, and will forsake me, and break my covenant which I have made with them. Then my anger shall be kindled against them in that day, and I will forsake them, and I will hide my face from them, and they shall be devoured, and many evils and troubles shall befall them...Now therefore write ye this song for you, and teach it the children of Israel: put it in their mouths, that this song may be a witness for me against the children of Israel. For when I shall have brought them into the land which I sware unto their fathers, that floweth with milk and honey...then will they turn unto other gods, and serve them, and provoke me, and break my covenant. And it shall come to pass, when many evils and troubles are befallen them, that this song shall testify against them as a witness; for it shall* *not be forgotten out of the mouths of their seed: for I know their imagination which they go about, even now, before I have brought them into the land which I sware. Moses therefore wrote this song the same day, and taught it the children of Israel. And he gave Joshua the son of Nun a charge, and said, Be strong and of a good courage: for thou shalt bring the children of Israel into the land which I sware unto them: and I will be with thee."* (Deuteronomy 31, 14-23)

Enoch: I sense that Moses decided to struggle no more and came to his senses as the servant of God.

TCG: Pay attention that everything written from that point onwards is just a recitation of what God had said to Moses, no interpretations anymore.

Enoch: With Moses naming Joshua as his successor, so there would be no quarrels over who is in charge of these people.

TCG: *"And it came to pass, when Moses had made an end of writing the words of this law in a book, until they were finished, That Moses commanded the Levites, which bare the ark of the covenant of the LORD, saying, Take this book of the law, and put it in the side of the ark of the covenant of the LORD your God, that it may be there for a witness against thee."* (Deuteronomy 31, 24-26)

Enoch: Moses was finally retiring.

TCG: Precisely; he has finished writing the laws of God and added those to the Ark of Covenant, finally doing his last project.

The Fiftieth Message - Joshua's Commission

Enoch: I have noticed that Moses has finally realised that he had no choice in the matter, and had to accept his fate which has prompted him to stop being an adversary to Joshua and undermining him. And then we noticed <u>Moses and Joshua singing together to the nation.</u>

TCG: Surprising, is it not?

Enoch: Indeed so: *"And Moses came and spake all the words of this song in the ears of the people, he, and Hoshea (Joshua) the son of Nun. And Moses made an end of speaking all these words to all Israel: And he said unto them, Set your hearts unto all the words which I testify among you this day, which ye shall command your children to observe to do, all the words of this law."* (Deuteronomy 32, 44-46)

So if everyone observes the law, they may prosper together, yes?

TCG: From this revelation, we continue towards the words of God to Moses: *"Get thee up into this mountain Abarim, unto mount Nebo, which is in the land of Moab, that is over against Jericho; and behold the land of Canaan, which I give unto the children of Israel for a possession: And die in the mount whither thou goest up, and be gathered unto thy people; as Aaron thy brother died in mount Hor, and was gathered unto his people: Because ye trespassed against me among the children of Israel at the waters of MeribahKadesh, in the wilderness of Zin; because ye sanctified me not in the midst of the children of Israel."* (Deuteronomy 32, 49-51)

Enoch: Feels to me that this event was mirroring what has happened in the Binding of Isaac: Moses was sacrificed for the sake of the Israelites and God's reasoning is vague.

TCG: And why do you feel that way? Did Abraham not tell Isaac what was about to happen? Did God not tell Moses what was about to happen? Did any of them hide the truth from one another?

Enoch: I find it cruel that Moses was not allowed to enter Canaan and was left to look upon it before dying.

TCG: True, but there are cryptic reasons as to why Moses must go; have you forgotten that Aaron went the same way?

Enoch: Yes, but Aaron was brought upon that mountain to be ridiculed.

TCG: Why would God ridicule Aaron?

Enoch: How was it not ridicule? He was brought on the mountain with the multitude of people, watching on as he was being stripped of his clothing.

TCG: That was not the intention.

Enoch: I am not a fool. The priests could have sewn a new suit of clothing for his son; Aaron was brought on the mountain to be executed.

TCG: What gave you that idea?

Enoch: Since he was also to blame for what has happened at MeiMeriba (Numbers 20); he might have been dressed in the orange jumpsuit of the time, who knows – but it seems to me that he was executed, and that was for shame for the Israelites – that was not a positive occurrence for them.

TCG: Maybe so, but that was not what it seemed to be.

Enoch: Moses' transgression at MeiMeriba is the same as Aaron's, hence why he was also brought on the mountain to die – that is execution.

TCG: We know for a fact that Moses knew he was to die once he went up the mountain. He knew fully well why Aaron was brought on the mountain and what has happened to him. What do you think could have happened?

Would Moses not try to persuade God to spare him, if only for the good he has done before to God and the people?

The Fifty-First Message - Was Moses the first prophet?

TCG: *"And this is the blessing, wherewith Moses the man of God blessed the children of Israel before his death."* (Deuteronomy 33, 1)

Enoch: These were the words of the author, not Moses'.

TCG: Very perceptive of you, but this quote was not brought to your attention for nothing – we must now learn the perception of "Moses the prophet" and all prophets who came afterwards (and before his time).

Enoch: What do you mean by that?

TCG: We know for a fact that Moses was the first prophet of Israel, so what is a prophet?

Enoch: A person who prophesies things that would happen, speaking the word of God.

TCG: Logical but incorrect.

Enoch: How did we know it was so?

TCG: This is what Man had learnt and understood; but what does it actually mean?

Enoch: I have no idea.

TCG: You have no idea how little you know about The Scriptures. Abraham was a prophet long before Moses was, it was even written so: *"Now therefore restore the man his wife; for he is a prophet, and he shall pray for thee, and thou shalt live: and if thou restore her not, know thou that thou shalt surely die, thou, and all that are thine."* (Genesis 20, 7) This was what God has said to the King of Grar, who has taken Abraham's wife Sarah to be his wife. According to God, Abraham was a prophet as well.

Enoch: Fine, so what is a prophet?

TCG: A person who receives a calling from God.

Enoch: For the rest of one's life?

TCG: Until the calling is over; remember Eldad and Meidad who prophesied in Numbers? That was still in Moses' time. Balaam himself was sent by God and once his calling was finished, he was killed by the Israelites. We must not also forget the dozens of prophets (including women) such as Miriam, Moses' sister and Isaiah's wife who was also called "Maiden and Prophet" during the reign of Ahaz, the king of Judea – many centuries later.

Enoch: So, was Moses also a prophet?

TCG: Yes, but we also understand what a prophet really is – "a person of God", and that is the classic prophecy which was then given more meaning in the future of The Scriptures.

Enoch: So Moses was a man of God before he died?

TCG: Precisely; you must understand that when you read about the subtleties of Moses' singing to the people and giving himself credit in the process: *"Moses commanded us a law, even the inheritance of the congregation of Jacob."* (Deuteronomy 33, 4) So even Moses calls it his own law, hence why it was called "Mosaic Law" in the traditions of the Israelites who then became Jews later on.

Enoch: I have also noticed that God was absent from this blessing.

TCG: It appears so; Moses was prophesying to each tribe based on that tribe's style and tradition.

Enoch: And then he needed to go up the mountain to die, how so?

The Fifty-Second Message - Without blessing, past or future

Enoch: I am content that the Israelites were not ignoring Moses' blessing towards each tribe, but I have also noticed the Tribe of Simeon received no blessing – How so?

TCG: It appears you cannot let sleeping dogs lie. Let us understand why there was no future for that tribe.

Enoch: What do you mean?

TCG: Do you remember what Shechem, son of Hamor (prince of Shechem – Modern-day Nabulus) had done unto Dinah?

Enoch: Yes, he raped her and her brother Simeon and Levi avenged her honour by killing all the men in the town, including Shechem and his father Hamor.

TCG: And do you remember how furious Jacob was, that he was now forced to flee from a possible vendetta by the neighbouring tribes?

Enoch: And that was the reason? What is your evidence for that?

TCG: When Jacob blessed his sons, he blessed everyone except Levi and Simeon. He never forgot how they made him flee and how their impulsiveness almost cost the lives of the entire tribe of Jacob: *"Simeon and Levi are brethren; instruments of cruelty are in their habitations. O my soul, come not thou into their secret; unto their assembly, mine honour, be not thou united: for in their anger they slew a man, and in their selfwill they digged down a wall. Cursed be their anger, for it was fierce; and their wrath, for it was cruel: I will divide them in Jacob, and scatter them in Israel."* (Genesis 49, 5-7)

Enoch: That is not a blessing <u>but a curse</u>.

TCG: The bottom line was that these tribes would be dispersed between the other tribes to cool their temper.

Enoch: But Moses did bless the Levites.

TCG: Because in all the blessings it was mentioned that all tribes joined Moses, including the Levites who cast the first stone. The Levites repented their sins.

Enoch: Because they cast the first stone, killing the idolaters who constructed the Golden Calf? What about Simeon then?

TCG: *"And when Phinehas, the son of Eleazar, the son of Aaron the priest, saw it, he rose up from among the congregation, and took a javelin in his hand; And he went after the man of Israel into the tent, and thrust both of them through, the man of Israel, and the woman through her belly. So the plague was stayed from the children of Israel."* (Numbers 25, 7-8) The head of the Simeonites and the priest of the Levites. The bottom line is, these transgressions in the future – what would they bring in your eyes?

Enoch: Am I supposed to know that?

TCG: In Sunday school, you were taught that the Levites dispersed among the rest of the tribes with no land of their own, so their role as the priesthood remain and they would not wish to become part of the "commoners". The Simeonites had a small stretch of land, an enclave within the larger land of the Judahites so that tribe would protect them instead. It could be that the Simeonites were the smallest and weakest tribe of all, so Moses' "blessing" did come to be.

Enoch: Now I understand why they were not blessed.

The Fifty-Third Message - Was Moses executed?

TCG: *"And Moses went up from the plains of Moab unto the mountain of Nebo, to the top of Pisgah, that is over against Jericho. And the LORD shewed him all the land of Gilead, unto Dan."* (Deuteronomy 34, 1)

Enoch: And why was Moses going up the mountain, if it were not to be executed without witnesses?

TCG: Moses knew he was on borrowed time; the people needed to enter Canaan.

Enoch: And in his presence, he was "in the way" – I do not understand this. Moses went up the mountain to so called "look over The Promised Land", so as to see the promise to his ancestors.

TCG: Moses knew it was his time to go; what did you expect the Israelites to do – leave him there and then continue into The Promised Land? It was his time to go.

Enoch: This reminds me of Hagar's fate in the desert; he lost his grace in the eyes of The Lord, and now was his time to die.

TCG: This outcome is not to your liking? Even Moses came to terms with it.

Enoch: This was a vile act, in my opinion. He was forced to go up the mountain to die – no different than Socrates who was forced to drink poison, even though Moses never tried to sway the Israelites from God (unlike Socrates): *"So Moses the servant of the LORD died there in the land of Moab, according to the word of the LORD."* (Deuteronomy 34, 5) It is even mentioned that he died there "according to the word of The Lord", how is that not execution?

TCG: That is what God does; He giveth life and He taketh life.

Enoch: That I understand, but Moses could have died within the camp, where everyone could see him die. The Israelites could have given him the same grace they have given Joseph – burying Moses' bones in The Promised Land.

TCG: Moses could have never been given the same grace and he could not die within the camp.

Enoch: But why not? Even Miriam was buried in front of the Israelites and was given that grace.

TCG: Moses was not Miriam.

Enoch: Was Miriam not a prophet as her brother, Moses? Did the people not love Moses as much as they loved Miriam (if not more)? Was Moses not "the chosen one"? We know that Aaron was never given that grace: he was stripped of his clothes which were then given to his son.

TCG: This tirade would not make God reverse his decision.

Enoch: Aaron himself was not buried either.

TCG: How can you be so sure of that?

Enoch: It is implied that he was not, as part of the degradation trip he was given. We know that Miriam died in their camp and was hence buried. We know that the ones who are "executed" then disappear. Nobody knows where they are buried (if at all). But the people loved Aaron and decided to mourn him for a whole month; a period of time which made no sense to keep in the wilderness. That was also their own volition to do so, not God's.

TCG: Notice the last honour Moses was given by the author from God: *"And Moses was an hundred and twenty years old when he died: his eye was not dim, nor his natural force abated."* (Deuteornomy 34, 7)

Enoch: So Moses was young for his years. God had given him an early grave for he paid him no heed when he hit the rock instead of speaking to it as he was ordered to. It is even mentioned that his burial site was nowhere to be found: *"And he buried him in a valley in the land of Moab, over against Bethpeor: but no man knoweth of his sepulchre unto this day."* (Deuteronomy 34, 6) Does this make sense to you? He was buried in front of BaalPhegor, the worst of the idols of the Israelites in the wilderness? Was there not an unprecedented massacre due to it?

TCG: I understand that I cannot persuade as to why Moses had to die or was "executed" in your words, but let me explain to you what God had intended.

Enoch: That intrigues me; please continue.

TCG: *"And the LORD said unto Moses, Lo, I come unto thee in a thick cloud, that the people may hear when I speak with thee, and believe thee for ever. And Moses told the words of the people unto the LORD."* (Exodus 19, 9) That was the moment God had made Moses his "lieutenant". From that moment Moses was the mouth of God and the Israelites believed that Moses was God's representative on earth. But, this "Gordian Knot" was to be severed between God and Moses. The people had to say their adieu to Moses and continue.

The people had to evolve

Enoch: But why like this? Why so heinously?

TCG: It is the same as cutting the umbilical cord; the people must now enter The Promised Land and conquer it. Moses "refused to go", hence he must have stepped out of the way.

Enoch: He found no reason to as he believed he could still contribute.

TCG: It was his time to go and let Joshua lead the people and conquer the land which would then become The Land of Israel: *"And Joshua the son of Nun was full of the spirit of wisdom; for Moses had laid his hands upon him: and the children of Israel hearkened unto him, and did as the LORD commanded Moses. And there arose not a prophet since in Israel like unto Moses, whom the LORD knew face to face, In all the signs and the wonders, which the LORD sent him to do in the land of Egypt to Pharaoh, and to all his servants, and to all his land, And in all that mighty hand, and in all the great terror which Moses shewed in the sight of all Israel."* (Deuteronomy 34, 9-12)

Enoch: So Moses was "in the way"?

TCG: Moses was undermining Joshua for years; had Moses come with Joshua to conquer the land, who would have listened to Joshua? He would then have been able to hinder and potentially alter God's plan for the Israelites.

Enoch: I understand God's intention now. But why with no witnesses? Why not take his bones for burial in The Promised Land?

TCG: Moses had to disappear so the Israelites would never visit his grave and ask for his grace, as he was God's lieutenant in their eyes (if not God). In his death, Moses presented "a danger" to Joshua's (and God's) authority: It would have been easier for both of them if Moses "disappeared".

Enoch: I understand. We have finished the Pentateuch!

Goodbye!

The Fifty-Fourth Message - Epilogue

Enoch: You mentioned that the Mosaic Law was not entirely given by God, that is to say, that Moses had developed some of its elements on his own.

TCG: When did I ever say that?

Enoch: You implied that it has happened so. There is a gap between what Moses had said and what God had intended more than once.

TCG: What matters is what <u>you understood from my teachings</u>. Moses understood that the people needed more pillars to create a strong nation and have a set of rules that made them different from everyone else, so they would stay a completely different nation on their own.

Enoch: What about the writings on the stones? Did Joshua give the order to do so or was it, God?

TCG: You tell me: *"And Moses with the elders of Israel commanded the people, saying, Keep all the commandments which I command you this day. And it shall be on the day when ye shall pass over Jordan unto the land which the LORD thy God giveth thee, that thou shalt set thee up great stones, and plaister them with plaister: And thou shalt write upon them all the words of this law, when thou art passed over, that thou mayest go in unto the land which the LORD thy God giveth thee, a land that floweth with milk and honey; as the LORD God of thy fathers hath promised thee. Therefore it shall be when ye be gone over Jordan, that ye shall set up these stones, which I command you this day, in mount Ebal, and thou shalt plaister them with plaister."* (Deuteronomy 27, 1-4) We know that Mount Gerizim and Mount Ebal were the Mounts of Blessing and Curse, respectively.

Enoch: So Joshua disobeyed?

TCG: Do you realise that this was **a new testament** between God and the Israelites?

Enoch: That I understand, but I am asking you.

TCG: Moses had asked that this testament would be done once the Israelites had crossed the Jordan, that is how we the readers interpret the divine decree which was given to Moses.

Enoch: And it never came to be?

TCG: Let us review, shall we: *"Moses my servant is dead; now therefore arise, go over this Jordan, thou, and all this people, unto the land which I do give to them, even to the children of Israel."* (Joshua 1, 2) Joshua has obeyed God's command, but nothing of the covenant and/or the sacrifices <u>once they crossed the Jordan</u>. On the second day, Joshua sent spies to Jericho and again – nothing of the sacrifice, after three days from crossing the Jordan. Was Joshua making any mention of Moses' wonders or commands for a testament? Nothing: *"And it came to pass, when all the people were clean passed over Jordan, that the LORD spake unto Joshua, saying, Take you twelve men out of the people, out of every tribe a man, And command ye them, saying, Take you hence out of the midst of Jordan...twelve stones, and ye shall carry them over with you, and leave them in the lodging place, where ye shall lodge this night...And Joshua said unto them, Pass over before the ark of the LORD your God into the midst of Jordan...That this may be a sign among you, that when your children ask their fathers in time to come...and these stones shall be for a memorial unto the children of Israel for ever. And the children of Israel did so as Joshua commanded, and took up twelve stones out of the midst of Jordan...For the priests which bare the ark stood in the midst of Jordan, until everything was finished that the LORD commanded Joshua to speak unto the people, according to all that Moses commanded Joshua...And it came to pass...that the ark of the LORD passed over, and the priests, in the presence of the people...About forty thousand prepared for war passed over before the LORD unto battle, to the plains of Jericho. On that day the LORD magnified Joshua in the sight of all Israel; and they feared him, as they feared Moses, all the days of his life. And the LORD spake unto Joshua, saying, Command the priests that bear the ark of the testimony, that they come up out of Jordan. Joshua therefore commanded the priests, saying, Come ye up* *out of Jordan. And it came to pass, when the priests that bare the ark of the covenant...And the people came up out of Jordan on the tenth day of the first month, and encamped in Gilgal...And those twelve stones, which they took out of Jordan, did Joshua pitch in Gilgal."* (Joshua 4, 1-20) Nothing about the sacrifices, no covenant, no testament, no altars – all was forgotten. God did not even make mention of that, as now know that Joshua was speaking with God directly as Moses did before him.

Enoch: How so? Why not?

TCG: We were reading Deuteronomy, not Joshua. We were just corroborating to see that what Moses said would happen and his commandments were kept once he died. But an altar was never erected for God. No new testament, no new covenant between God the Israelites, as Moses intended.

Enoch: So it was never Joshua's intention to keep Moses' promise?

TCG: Precisely; once he killed the king of Ai, God had demanded nothing of Joshua and never made mention of what Moses had told Joshua to do. Joshua himself knew how to make the distinction between Mosaic Law and God's Law and that is exactly what he has done: *"Then Joshua built an altar unto the LORD God of Israel in mount Ebal, As Moses the servant of the LORD commanded the children of Israel, as it is written in the book of the law of Moses, an altar of whole stones, over which no man hath lift up any iron: and they offered thereon burnt offerings unto the LORD, and sacrificed peace offerings. And he wrote there upon the stones a copy of the law of Moses, which he wrote in the presence of the children of Israel."* (Joshua 8, 30-32) As you can see "law of Moses", not God's.

Enoch: That makes sense; he did need to fight first.

TCG: God met with Joshua every day before Joshua's battles. Because Joshua felt compelled to follow Moses' order, he decided to erect that altar to God. But he made the distinction between Mosaic Law and God's Law as you can see for yourself. This is why the book is called "Deuteronomy" which means "The Second Law".

Enoch: So what is the second law?

TCG: An addition to what God had said; an addendum of sorts. This was the first time the law was written and not oral.

Enoch: I am shocked to hear that; I never felt that way towards it.

TCG: But the ancients did know the difference, hence why they called it The Second Law.

Enoch: Fine, but why was the Mosaic Law not given to the elders or Phineas, Moses' grand-nephew?

TCG: God had given the power to Joshua through Moses; Moses was the one who ordained Joshua to be his successor. Yes, Joshua naturally did not teach the Israelites about the Law, but the oral tradition remained while the Levites continued teaching the written word to the people in later years.

Enoch: So who was it passed on to?

TCG: The beauty of the Mosaic Law and God's Law is that every educated person knew the rules; these rules were then applied for the future of the subsequent kingdoms in Canaan and were applied within the other Abrahamic religions, which has given rise to modern society which on the one hand lives by rules created by the ancients, revised to accommodate the values post revolutions, the separation of Religion and State and the promotion of critical and free-thinking.

Enoch: But society remains a tad conservative, no?

TCG: Observant would be a better word for it.

Monologue

The messages given to me by The Celestial Guide were not something I knew prior. I tried calling him again and again but he never returned to me. I have made my own research based on the system which he taught me and found more places which had solidified my understanding of the Mosaic Law and how much my guide was right.

I find it marvellous to know that the more I added details, the more I fixate the guide's perception of it all. For example: when Abraham tells God that he should not smite Sodom and Gomorrah if there may be just people living in it, it astounds me that Abraham had dared to question God's decree for the cities, thinking he is somewhat of his "equal".

I was thinking to myself how is it possible to have this type of morals? What did Abraham learn? How to distinguish between good and bad? Perhaps it is embedded in us. We do know that his understanding of what good and bad was different than what we find as good and bad in modern times. He did give away his wife twice: Once to Pharaoh and once to the King of Grar; in both cases, he turned out wealthy, but we also know that Man had to be cunning and conniving in those days to succeed.

But the question remains – who taught him this? Who showed him the way? Who explained everything there was to explain to him about life?

When we hear and follow God's commandments, we find out that this paving of the way does not exist. So was Abraham also given guidance by such "beings" and "guides"?

I wonder. Was it possible that the author of Genesis did not know of such beings and guides or just did not understand anything about it...? Was it possible that he knew and decided to evade possible questions about it?

There has to be an explanation!

-Enoch

-FIN-